Northern Comanche war chief, Broken Blade, won't rest until justice is served against the bloodthirsty renegades who brutally murdered a woman of his tribe. But Blade never counted on finding a blonde beauty, bound and naked, in his enemy's tepee.

Kidnapped from a train by a ruthless Indian outlaw, Amanda Murchison finds herself scared and alone until she is rescued by a bronzed warrior who appears every bit as dangerous as the man holding her hostage. But what frightens Amanda most is her passionate response to his raw sexual nature.

Unbridled In Buckskins
Copyright © 2022 Robin Gideon
ISBN: 978-1-4874-3627-8
Cover art by Martine Jardin

Published by Extasy Books

Look for us online at:
www.eXtasybooks.com

Unbridled In Buckskins

By

Robin Gideon

Dedication

To Keith . . . who kept me sane through the move and had the sense to say: "Sometimes a good cry can make the soul feel better."

CHAPTER ONE

His name was Broken Blade, and his most immediate goal was to stay alive long enough to kill Blue Elk. The odds of success weren't in Blade's favor, but then, on this particularly savage quest, they never had been. Not even at the very beginning, when the identity of the murderers was not yet known to Blade, the leader of the Northern Comanche.

Her name had been Summer Without Rain, and her body had been found eight days earlier on the southern banks of the Misserling River. Her corpse was naked, and the suffering she had experienced prior to death was as evident as if the defilement had been written in words. She had been kidnapped — a not unusual fate for young women among the tribes of the plains. What was unusual was the viciousness of the gang rape and murder.

That ruled out the usual enemies of the Northern Comanche, namely the Cheyenne to the north, the Kiowa and Sioux to the southeast, and the Sauk and Fox farther to the east and north. While something significantly less than consensual romantic encounters was not uncommon among the Plains Indians, gang rape followed by murder was considered by all the tribes as an abomination.

It had taken less than thirty-six hours to determine that Summer Without Rain had been abducted by Blue Elk's ragtag band of renegades, killers, and outcasts. They weren't a tribe, or even a clan, per se, in as much as their numbers were less than twenty, and all were braves who had been banished from their tribes. Blue Elk, along with his younger brother,

Dog, had banded together with outcasts from the neighboring Cheyenne and Kiowa tribes to form a formidable fighting force of thieves and outlaws.

On the Great Plains, being banished from one's tribe meant a death sentence, as often as not. Living without the protection of the tribe made a man vulnerable to all manner of hostility from any number of tribes. And the white man, it seemed, had never been one to miss an opportunity to kill a defenseless Indian.

Blue Elk understood this and used it to his advantage, assembling braves who possessed a great regard for their own life but no regard for anyone else's. Even before the hostilities between the Northern and Southern states had turned into open warfare, Blue Elk had been terrorizing whites and Indians alike along the Arkansas River, robbing and pillaging, killing indiscriminately, raping whenever possible.

Summer Without Rain had been young and innocent when she was abducted. A virgin, she had been wistfully looking forward to the coming winter, when she would at last be old enough to accept a Northern Comanche brave as a husband — and she had her eye on several young braves who met her idea of bravery and masculine beauty.

Her death — violent, sexual, and completely unnecessary — was an affront to the nearly one thousand Northern Comanche, and it was up to Broken Blade, the Chief of War, to uphold the honor of the tribe and see that justice was served. In this case, nothing less than death would do.

He had chosen to go after Blue Elk alone. To catch Blue Elk, Blade had to ride deep into Cheyenne country. The more riders there were, the greater the chances of being seen.

At least riding alone, should a wandering Cheyenne clan see the tracks of his horse, they would be less inclined to assume a raiding war party was in their territory. Braves often got lost traveling from one encampment to another, or white men from one city to another. But a single rider wasn't a threat. If there were many riders it would constitute a threat that the Cheyenne would need to address if they were to maintain their dignity. The Cheyenne were nothing if not proud and dignified — and more than willing to defend their territory against all trespassers.

If the Cheyenne captured Blade, he would either be killed, or sold back to the Northern Comanche for a hefty ransom, using the universal currency among the tribes — horses. If the Kiowa caught him, he would be killed immediately. The Kiowa had lost many horses and many skirmishes to warriors under Blade's command. The Kiowa wanted revenge, and the longer they had to wait to taste it, the more they hungered for it. And if Blue Elk and his vicious band of cutthroats captured Blade, he would surely be tortured before he was killed.

Which meant Blade had to sneak into Blue Elk's camp, kill him, then sneak back out — all without drawing any attention to himself and his activities whatsoever.

A bitter smile pulled at his mouth. This time, doing the honorable thing was probably going to cost him his life.

They're going to kill me.

Amanda Murchison tested the strips of rawhide surrounding her wrists and ankles. Like all the other times, she found the leather unyielding, her bindings attached to four wooden stakes hammered into the ground.

But before they kill me, they are going to make me suffer. How many are there? A dozen? Maybe more? They'll all take their turn with me . . . then they'll kill me.

Hours earlier, Amanda had been aboard the northbound train, headed for Colorado City, where she hoped to find a new job teaching children to read and write and do math. When the train stopped midway between stations, she hadn't understood at first that things had gone desperately wrong.

But then Blue Elk and his band of renegade outlaws raced through the four passenger coaches, pistols blasting and knives slashing, killing everyone in sight without hesitation or mercy.

Only Amanda's life had been spared — and she knew why. Blue Elk had decided she was too beautiful to be killed outright. He had said as much when he introduced himself with mock formality, bowing low as a courting gentleman would . . . except there had been blood on the enormous blade of the knife he held.

That had been only a few hours earlier. To Amanda, it seemed like a lifetime.

Laughter came from outside the tepee. Blue Elk and his men were drinking whiskey and having a good time. It had been a profitable day for them. Several of the passengers were carrying their life's savings on their way to Colorado City, intent on setting up a new life. Amanda knew she was scheduled to be their entertainment for the evening . . . but first they were going to get good and liquored up.

Sounds of movement outside caught her attention. A moment later, Blue Elk stepped into the tepee. He was short and dark-skinned. The small fire in the center of the tepee cast flickering light on his naked chest.

"Are you ready to honor me?" Blue Elk asked, slurring his words slightly.

Amanda gasped softly when Blue Elk dropped to his knees beside her. For several seconds, his gaze caressed her as he fondled the naked fullness of her heavy breasts. When he put his big palm upon her stomach, she flinched.

"P-please don't hurt me," she said, her eyes squeezed tightly shut.

His hand, heavily callused, slid up her stomach, pausing briefly at the under-curve of her breast before he cupped the firm mound.

"Nice," Blue Elk said quietly. "You have a body that pleases me." He squeezed her breast with one hand as he took a drink of whiskey from the bottle with the other. "If you are good to me and make me happy, perhaps I will let you live." He paused, wiping his mouth with the back of his hand. "I have never seen a body as beautiful as yours." He caught her nipple and pinched hard enough to make her wince in pain. "Do you have a rich father, yellow eyes? Maybe I can sell you back. Are you rich?"

Amanda opened her eyes and looked up at her captor. "No," she said softly. "I'm not rich. And I don't have much family, and none of them are rich."

Blue Elk released her breast, sat on the backs of his heels, and looked down at Amanda, trussed up securely for his pleasure. His gaze trailed slowly down her nakedness until it reached the small, triangular patch of hair at the apex of her thighs.

"What is this?" He caught several of the curly strands between his forefinger and thumb, tugging on the pubic hair hard enough to pluck several strands.

Amanda made a whimpering sound in her throat, both in pain and humiliation.

He scowled disdainfully and shook his head in condescension. "You yellow eyes are all cursed. You know nothing worth knowing."

Blue Elk tried to take another swallow of whiskey but discovered that the bottle was empty. "I need more whiskey, yellow eyes, then I will be back for you."

He stood and looked down at Amanda. She shivered at the way his gaze roamed over her nudity. There wasn't a trace of human warmth in his dark expression. "Blue Elk is first with you." He tossed the empty bottle to the opposite side of the tepee. "When the sun comes up, you will not be so pretty." He grinned, showing several missing teeth. "My braves are true warriors. To have someone like you will make their blood run hot. That is good for them . . . but bad for you, yellow eyes."

Blue Elk was laughing softly as he left his tepee.

Blade saw the first sentry long before he even got close to the renegade camp. It was impossible to tell whether the young man was Kiowa or Cheyenne, judging by his coarse buckskin shirt and the leggings that had seen much use.

The answer was of little interest to Blade. What he did care about was the man's attention, and at present, as he leaned back against a solitary elm tree, most of that attention was focused on a bottle of amber liquid in his right hand. Transiently, Blade wondered what the young warrior had done to get kicked out of his tribe. Aware that it had to have been something heinous helped ease Blade's conscience.

Blade had stripped down for the attack to nothing but his buckskin breechclout, moccasins, and weapons. On his left hip, in a cross-draw holster, was a .36 caliber revolver. Attached to the same wide leather belt, on his right hip, was an antler-handled knife with a heavy twelve-inch blade. The knife had belonged to Blade's father. Upon proving himself to be a man of honor, a hunter and provider, and a warrior, Blade had earned the right to carry it.

Extracting the knife slowly from its sheath, he made his way cautiously through the tall grass, moving ever closer to the sentry's post and to the four tepees beyond that, his progress as silent as a stalking cougar's.

The sentry's head was tilted back, and he was pouring whiskey down his throat when he died. He did not make more than a brief gurgling sound as death claimed him. Blade was already moving forward through the shadows when the sentry's strong heart beat its last.

Blade continued on. He heard the raucous laughter of the braves around the campfire, their words clear enough that he could make out the languages. As was so often the case when tribes had overlapping territory, the languages tended to blend one into another. He recognized Kiowan words, as well as words from the Algonkian family language, which encompassed the Cheyenne. A grim smile touched Blade's mouth. He was in the right place.

Movement to his right, from the one tepee set aside from the other three, caught his attention. A warrior of medium height stepped out of a tepee, pulling the cork on a bottle as he walked. Blade watched, appalled as the warrior tilted the bottle back, drinking and walking at the same time.

Once, a dozen years earlier while attending college, Blade had foolishly filled his champagne glass and was walking and drinking. His geology professor, the host of the gathering, pulled him aside and, in quiet but granite-hard tones, informed Blade that no gentleman ever walked and drank liquor simultaneously. It simply wasn't done.

Blade never made that offense against propriety again.

As the warrior let the bottle dangle from his hand at his side, light settled on his swarthy features. It was Blue Elk. There could be no doubt about it.

The urge to rush forward, pistol in hand, and settle the score was almost overpowering for Blade. For a moment — he dared not do it any longer — he squeezed his eyes tightly shut and searched within for the discipline he knew was necessary. Any fool could commit suicide and perhaps, just maybe, do something good in the process. But a wise warrior fought only when he had to, then he fought with stealth and cunning and an eye toward surviving the battle, not with foolhardy bravado that only created dead warriors and grieving widows.

It was then, as Blade was harnessing the personal discipline that was the hallmark of his personality, that Blue Elk spoke.

"I come back to give you what's left of this bottle," Blue Elk said, much more loudly than was necessary to carry on the still night air. "I am going to my tepee now. Tomorrow, we will talk."

There was a general uproar of bawdy laughter from the more than dozen men surrounding the campfire, all of them in various stages of inebriation. Blade didn't wait to consider what the laughter meant.

Though he was a tall man by any standard, when he moved, he made no sound, his moccasins seemingly gliding over the prairie grass, the muscles in his chest and back moving beneath his sun-darkened skin like the muscles of a mountain lion rippling beneath velvet-soft tawny fur.

Blade slipped through the open entrance flap to Blue Elk's tepee without breaking stride, the razor-sharp knife in his steady right hand, his heart pounding but his confidence soaring. Soon, Blue Elk would be dead, and he would have avenged the tribe known as the Northern Comanche, and the weight of responsibility pressing on his soul would be lifted.

And that's when he saw the pale-skinned woman, spread-eagled in the tepee, her arms and legs outstretched, tied to wooden stakes that had been pounded into the earth through the buffalo robes beneath her.

The breath caught in Blade's throat, and his teeth clenched. The warrior in him whispered that she wasn't of his tribe, and since she wasn't, was not his responsibility. Besides, any involvement she might have in his life would create an infinite number of complications regarding his escape once the pesky problem of Blue Elk's continued good health was dealt with.

But there was another part of Blade's body and soul, that part of him instilled by an innate sense of decency and the knowledge of universal rights and wrongs, a part that had been inculcated in him by his Northern Comanche elders as well as the Jesuit priests, who silently said with quiet conviction that to let this poor, unfortunate woman suffer at the hands of Blue Elk's band of savage misfits would be a crime against humanity.

And if Father McMurphy had lectured endlessly on any subject, it was the need for good men to uphold the dictates of humanity.

The woman turned her head, and when she saw him, her eyes became enormous. It appeared as though she was about to say something, and Blade reacted with catlike speed. He was on his knees, a broad palm clamped over the woman's mouth to silence anything she might say.

Though he continued to hold the knife in his hand, he put his index finger to his lips in the universally recognized hand-symbol for silence. He looked straight into the woman's eyes when he nodded. Seconds ticked by — seconds he didn't have to spare — before the woman nodded.

Blade removed his hand from her mouth and leapt to his feet. He was back near the entrance, opposite the woman, an instant later. He knew if she made a sound, if she did anything at all that would indicate things were different than a few minutes earlier when Blue Elk left the tepee, then Blade's bold, impromptu plan for revenge would be for naught . . . and his own death would have accomplished nothing.

No longer directly above her, Blade experienced the full magnitude of her nudity, of the awesome natural splendor of her body. She was pale-skinned, not particularly tall, with tapering thighs, curved hips, a waist neither slender nor ample . . . leading to breasts that caused a man's heart to leap in his chest. The sheer, extravagant size and shape of her breasts caused Blade's heart to pound. Heavy, full, deliciously rounded mounds of feminine extravagance guaranteed to entice the eyes and . . .

Blade closed his eyes for a second and shook his head, as

he often did to clear his thoughts and calm his mind. This was not the time to be rendered catatonic from a woman's beauty—especially not for a man whose experience with women, Caucasian or Indian, had caused countless tongues to wag from Sioux Falls to Denver City to St. Louis. When he opened his eyes an instant later, the knife in his hand was of maximum importance; the woman, bound naked with leather cords tied to stakes was of fleeting, insignificant interest.

He heard Blue Elk's footsteps. The sound of them pleased Blade. It told him the warrior he hunted, the man who had caused such blind fear in the territory, had lost the sharp edge of his perceptions. Blue Elk had, like so many before him, come to believe savagery and murderous indifference to others' sufferings was the same as having power. Earning the fear of others was infinitely easier though far less valuable than earning their respect . . . but Blue Elk didn't understand that distinction.

Blade looked at the woman once again, her face ghastly pale in the flickering light of the small fire. With his left hand, he motioned over his eyes, closing them. Then he pointed to her. To his pleasure, she immediately closed her eyes and turned her face away from the tepee entrance, exactly as he had wanted her to.

In a warrior's life, there were some things that had to be done that should never be witnessed by a woman. Blade understood this, and even though the laws of his tribe didn't extend to the white man's world, his heart said it should.

Blue Elk bent low to step into his tepee. Once inside, he stood erect and looked down at his naked and helpless captive. "I'm going to stuff your pussy with so much cock you won't believe it. I'm going to fuck you and then—"

He was dead a heartbeat later, and Blade's only regret was that he had allowed the vile murderer and rapist the chance to speak one last time.

Easing the corpse to the opposite side of the fire, away from the blonde woman, Blade turned the body face-down, then grabbed a buffalo skin from the floor of the tepee and tossed it over Blue Elk's bloody head and shoulders. A jugular vein, when severed, created massive bleeding.

When Blade looked again at the woman, her face was still turned away, but her breasts moved with her rapid-fire breathing and her eyes were closed. She was scared. Scared out of her mind. But she had shown the good sense to do exactly as she had been instructed and hadn't made a sound.

In a soft tone he hoped was comforting, Blade spoke in the flawless English that had been taught to him by his mother and by an assortment of priests and university professors. "Please, no matter what you do, don't make any noise. I'm not here to hurt you. I promise you that."

The woman turned her head and looked straight at Blade with eyes the size of saucers. For the first time, Blade could tell just how young Blue Elk's voluptuous captive was, and it shocked him. She might be out of her teen years, but if she was, it wasn't by much.

In a hushed, rather incredulous tone, she asked, "Y-you . . . you speak English?"

"Quite well, actually." He smiled. "My name is Broken Blade."

"But you're . . ." The remainder of the sentence remained unspoken, but not mistaken.

"An Indian? Yes. To be more specific, a Northern Comanche. However . . ." He smiled charmingly, even though every instinct in him was to run like the wind and let this yellow eyes squaw fend for herself. "You have a name? Can you walk?"

"My name is Amanda, and I can run if you'll just cut me loose," the woman said. Then, despite the poor light inside the tepee, she blushed and added, "And if you could find me some clothes, I'd be ever so grateful."

The civility of the words, in stark contrast to the visual image of a voluptuous Caucasian woman trussed up naked inside a tepee, was enough to make all the internal gyroscopes that kept Blade's thinking on the level suddenly begin to tilt. In a flash, his glinting knife cut the leather thongs binding the woman's wrists and ankles.

"Listen to me carefully." Blade did everything he could to keep from looking at the woman's breasts, which, he noted with a connoisseur's eye for detail, were nothing less than extravagantly splendid. "If you want, you can follow me. But you must remain absolutely silent the entire time. You must keep running. No matter what happens, keep running and say nothing. Is that clear?"

She had an arm folded crosswise over her bosom in a failing and unintentionally erotic attempt to hide their naked fullness. Her other hand was between her legs to hide her sex. Blade would have liked to pretend he hadn't noticed the woman's allure, but his libido was as fine-tuned as the precision watches coming out of Switzerland that kept perfect time. Circumstances be damned; a beautiful woman, his body said, was something to pay attention to.

"Well?" he demanded, keeping his voice low when she didn't immediately respond. The majority of his anger was directed at himself since he couldn't keep his eyes off her body or his thoughts off vaguely licentious notions of what pleasures would be his should he slide his hips between those shapely thighs, and . . .

"I won't make a sound. I promise you that." Her blue eyes were filled with sincerity, and her naked breasts trembled enticingly despite her best efforts to conceal them with a single slender arm. "Please, take me with you. Take me away from this."

Blade nodded, then turned away from the woman. He

couldn't look at her any longer without a certain part of him, which he'd never had much control over in the first place if the truth should ever be known, standing up and paying rather obvious attention to the blonde woman. Considering the fact that he was wearing only a buckskin breechclout, his intemperate thoughts and wayward body part would be impossible to conceal.

Using his knife, Blade sliced a long hole in the back of Blue Elk's tepee, crawled through, then helped the woman through.

Despite his better judgment, despite all the reasons he had for distrusting white people he did not personally know, Broken Blade, War Chief of the Northern Comanche, took the woman's hand and started into a ground-eating dogtrot he could keep up for hours. His only concern was how long the barefooted, naked white woman could keep it up, and how much danger she would put him in because of her deficiency.

To the surprise of a man who had lived in jeopardy literally every day of his life, the additional danger of that woman in his life seemed a very small price to pay.

CHAPTER TWO

A manda kept up with the tall Indian, but she wasn't certain how much longer she could continue the pace. What would he do if she slowed him down? Abandon her to the band of cutthroats who had abducted her from the train, or silently kill her himself so that she wouldn't betray his escape plans?

At first, it had hurt to run barefooted through the tall buffalo grass, but now her feet just felt numb. She hadn't been outdoors without shoes on since she was a child.

Blade's enormous left hand was wrapped around her right wrist. Once, when Amanda tripped, he simply hauled her upright without breaking stride. She suspected he could snap her wrist with very little effort if he felt so inclined.

She was wildly embarrassed at her own nudity and grateful that Blade, running in front of her and dragging her along behind him, wasn't in a position to leisurely ogle her. With each hurried stride, Amanda's heavy breasts bounced and swayed erratically, making it impossible for her to forget for even a second that she was completely naked with an Indian warrior, who, she knew without any doubts whatsoever, was a killer. A cold-blooded killer . . . who spoke English with a precision that could only come from a formal education. But he had the bronzed skin and wore moccasins and a buckskin breechclout of a Plains Indian.

She stumbled and this time completely lost her footing so that for several steps Blade dragged her along behind him.

"Wait!" Amanda gasped, scrambling to get to her feet,

14

gulping in air. "I c-can't go much farther."

"My horse is less than fifty yards from here. You can make it that far," Blade replied with only the faintest trace of sympathy in his tone.

Amanda looked at him appraisingly, stunned that, though she was quite winded, he wasn't even breathing particularly hard. The broad expanse of his naked chest had become moist with perspiration, and it reflected the pale moonlight in a distinctly erotic manner. But as her gaze caressed the relaxed muscles in Blade's naked chest, his dark eyes locked on her breasts that wiggled tautly with her panting breaths.

"Lead the way," Amanda said, suddenly aware of Blade's scrutiny and feeling decidedly uneasy because of it. "I promise, I won't slow you down."

By the time they reached Blade's pinto, a thick-chested mare with patches of black, chestnut brown, and white, Amanda was beginning to wonder whether the man who had rescued her from certain death ever got exhausted.

As they neared the mare, the animal lifted her head and whinnied in greeting. Blade rubbed her nose to calm her. Their emotional bond was marrow deep.

"You're going to have to carry two of us, Tikki," Blade said to his mare as he picked up the reins from where they dangled to the prairie grass. "Be a good girl and don't complain too much."

The horse was a four-legged arsenal. Attached to a very abbreviated saddle on the left side of the mare was a sheath holding a bow and a quiver full of arrows. In a saddle scabbard on the right side of the horse was a lever-action rifle.

"Tell me you know how to ride," Blade said, turning sharply toward her.

Crossing an arm over her breasts and placing a hand between her legs, she nodded, grateful that her father had insisted she learn.

"At least I've got that bit of luck working for me," Blade murmured. He put a moccasin-shod foot into a rawhide stirrup and swung up into the saddle with deceptively lithe grace, considering the size of the man. Once in the saddle, he kicked his foot out of the stirrup and reached a hand down to assist her. "Come on, we'd better put some miles between us and those men. They're not going to take kindly to me killing Blue Elk."

Trying to tell herself there was nothing of her body he hadn't already seen and that she had much more pressing problems at the moment than trying to maintain some semblance of modesty, Amanda put her hand into Blade's outstretched one, eased her bare foot into the stirrup, and pulled herself up onto the mare's back. She slipped her arms around his waist, feeling the warmth and wetness of his abdomen beneath her palms. Feeling, too, the tempting sensation of his muscular back, heated with exertion and rock solid with muscle, against the mounds of her breasts and tantalized nipples that were annoyingly sensitive under the circumstance.

"Let's go, Tikki." Blade kept his voice low as he touched his heels to the mare's ribs. The horse broke into an easy canter that could eat up the miles without exhausting either horse or rider. Glancing over his shoulder, Blade looked at Amanda and smiled. "I'm sorry to say it, but that bare bottom of yours is going to be red as an apple by sunup."

Amanda closed her eyes as the blush of embarrassment crept swiftly up her neck, coloring her cheeks and ears to a rosy hue.

The girl's got courage, and she knows not to complain.

Blade walked Tikki into a cool stream, fed by melting mountain snows. They were now miles away from the corpse that had at one time been a heartless monster named Blue Elk. Though Blade had kept the pace steady, he didn't travel as fast as he could, choosing instead to show some sympathy for Amanda's naked backside, and for Tikki, who was carrying extra weight.

Of all the plains and mountain Indians, perhaps none were greater equestrians than the Comanche tribes. By the time a Northern Comanche boy was five, a girl eight, they were riding by themselves. But even with his own lifetime of experience on horseback, should he have a bare ass while riding at a canter for very long his flesh would be rubbed raw, his testicles flaming red.

That was one of the purposes of wearing a six-foot-long breechclout made of butter-soft buckskin. By folding the leather beneath the rider, it provided a cushioning and several protective layers of leather between man and horse.

"We'll go at a walk now," Blade said over his shoulder. "How are you holding up?"

"I'm a little sore." After a pause of several seconds, apparently not wanting to appear ungrateful, she added, "But I'll be fine . . . thanks to you. That man . . . he . . . he was going to—"

"Don't think about that now," Blade said quickly. "He can't hurt you anymore. Blue Elk's days of hurting women are over. And do you want to know something? I feel pretty damned good about that."

Tikki dipped her head, wanting a drink of the cool water, and Blade let her. Sitting loose in the saddle, at last convinced that the escape had been accomplished and that sudden death was a most unlikely event, he was disturbingly aware of the woman's breasts against his naked back.

When he had to concentrate on making good their escape, it was easy to focus on the very real threats he faced, but now that their safety was assured, his mind, body, and libido could leisurely take in the deliciously evocative tactile stimulation received when a very voluptuous woman was riding double with him without wearing any clothes.

Blade's slumbering cock woke and began to lengthen inside his breechclout.

"Would you mind if we stopped? Just for a couple minutes?" Amanda asked, her voice very soft.

Realizing that the best thing he could do was put some distance between himself and the naked woman he had rescued, Blade quickly agreed. He walked Tikki to the opposite side of the stream and found a place where the grass was thick and green. "Stay where you're at."

Blade leaned back to kick his right leg over Tikki's neck and was immediately aware of the extravagant mounds of Amanda's breasts against his back, the fullness and firmness of which sent an intensely erotic electric shock shooting through his body. Before his moccasins hit the cool, moist grass, Blade could feel his sexual willpower begin to crumble.

In a voice that suddenly sounded quite strained, he reached up with both hands and said with as much indifference as he could muster, "Let me help you down."

Gripping her naked waist just above her hips, he helped Amanda off his horse. His brain screamed savagely at the injustice of being so close to an amazingly voluptuous, stunningly beautiful young woman who just happened to be completely naked . . . and probably shouldn't be seduced when hours earlier she had narrowly eluded gang-rape and execution.

The instant Amanda's feet touched the grass, Blade released her and turned sharply away. He wasn't a man with much experience in sexual temperance.

"We'll stay here ten minutes. The water here is crystal clean if you're thirsty."

Amanda whispered a grateful "Thank you" as she headed toward the stream a few feet away.

From his buckskin pack on Tikki, Blade removed a work

shirt, simple in design and without the adornments of quills and beadwork his war shirt had. The shirt would be extremely large on Amanda, though he doubted the tails would come down far enough to protect her buttocks from the ravages of naked horseback riding. After considering his options for a moment, Blade came to the conclusion that the only other article of clothing he could offer her was some of his own breechclout.

"I have something for you." Blade held the shirt in his hands.

Early in the spring, after the squaws had stretched and softened the hide, Blade had sewn the two leather halves of the shirt together himself. The act of self-reliance had created something of a scandal within the Northern Comanche tribe since sewing was in the exclusive realm of the squaws. The fact that a war chief of Broken Blade's esteem should be sewing his own clothing had not sat well with tribal elders, and Blade was given a stern warning that he should pick a wife soon . . . or one or more wives would be picked for him.

His older brother's widow, Moon Will Shine, was now through with her mourning, and as the next oldest male sibling of the family, Blade was honor-bound to provide for her. That did not necessarily mean he had to take her as his wife, but such accommodations were quite common among the Northern Comanche.

Amanda approached, the ineffectual arm across her breasts making her appear more naked than if she weren't trying to hide herself. The hand between her thighs hid her sex but left on display the erotically sweeping curve of her hips. Blade did all he could to not stare. The sun wouldn't come up for another hour, and with the sunrise he would have a fully illuminated view of Amanda's naked perfection, which, he suspected, would be irresistible.

Never in his life had Blade's willpower been so tested.

Though he was a man of many extraordinary talents, harnessing his libido had never one he could boast about. There were, however, any number of women who could testify to his ability to sensually entertain for literally hours and hours on end.

As he handed her the buckskin shirt, he shrugged. "At least it's something." He tried to sound casual, as though Amanda's nudity left him unaffected. It didn't, but he felt the need to pretend. "It'll be big on you."

Amanda took the shirt, and in order for her to pull the soft leather over her head, abandoned her efforts at hiding her breasts. In a tiny corner of Blade's mind, he could hear Father McMurphy's voice whispering that a gentleman would turn his back when confronted with such enticing but nevertheless forbidden temptations.

Despite his best intentions to the contrary, Blade was unable to turn his back on her when she pulled the buckskin shirt over her head. Somewhere in the process an arm got trapped in a sleeve, or perhaps she hadn't quite positioned the garment properly for her head to slip through the sizable neck hole. However it worked out, for fully thirty glorious seconds, her head and arms were inside the buckskin shirt and the rest of her body was gleaming naked in the moonlight for his leisurely, appreciative inspection. Unbidden, his cock began swelling.

Erections were not uncommon for a man as virile as Blade.

As the leather came free and slithered down over ripe breasts and slender arms slipped into sleeves made for much larger limbs, Blade turned his back.

"Thank you," Amanda said, "for allowing me my modesty."

Blade looked at her again, and for a moment, the tightness in his throat was so intense he couldn't speak. He looked directly into her pale blue eyes, searching for some sign of theatricality, some indication that she wasn't really as sweetly innocent and grateful as she appeared.

Though the history of his people and life's circumstances had, in many ways, made Blade a cynical man . . . there was nothing in Amanda's eyes that suggested she was anything other than a very frightened woman who was extremely grateful to the man who had saved her life.

The shirt came down to the middle of her thighs. Though the buckskin concealed Amanda's sex, the sight of her white legs, naked and beautiful beneath the unadorned hem, was the very definition of feminine temptation.

After clearing his throat, Blade said, "If you'll give me a moment, I think I can create a little something else that should make it more comfortable to ride." He smiled, and his shoulders once again moved in a fluid shrug. "It won't be much, but it should help."

Amanda turned her back to Blade but didn't take so much as a single step away. In a voice barely audible, she said, "You've been so kind to me, how will I ever repay you . . ."

Blade squeezed his eyes shut for a moment as shockingly intemperate wayward thoughts of repayment by way of sexual satisfaction slithered through his brain. For the tenth time since discovering Blue Elk had a captive in his tepee, Blade had to remind himself that Amanda was a young woman who had been kidnapped, and the last thing in the world she needed was for a lusty man to turn his amorous attentions upon her.

Ignoring her feminine charms was the gentlemanly thing to do. Father McMurphy most assuredly would have agreed with Blade's decision. But then, the good father was strong when it came to temptations of the flesh.

However, it was thoroughly and completely impossible for a man of Broken Blade's well-honed libertine sensibilities to ignore the eroticism of the woman he was with.

He waited for a moment, looking at Amanda's motionless

back while his mind whirled like a tornado. Her blonde hair reflected the sparse moonlight with a golden glow, and the urge to take her into his arms was suffocating in its intensity.

With dispatch, Blade's hands did the bidding of his better judgment. He unbuckled the wide leather belt, holding his revolver and holster at one hip and a sheath and knife at the other, and dropped them to the ground. Then he unknotted the slender braided cord surrounding his waist, and instantly the soft buckskin fell to the grass at his feet. His arousal, half-formed and yet already impressive in both length and girth, sprang free and swung away from his loins.

Don't look at her! Don't! Don't!

His efforts were futile. Amanda represented a feminine magnetism that was much stronger than his willpower. In a vain effort to maintain some semblance of self-control, he consciously called forth bigotry.

She's a yellow eyes!

This last thought was so ludicrous it nearly made him laugh. He had seduced far too many 'yellow eyes' to make any credible argument that he found something unseemly about the Caucasian race. The fact that his mother, who Blade adored with the devotion given only to saints, was a highborn Englishwoman was conveniently forgotten during this brief but riotous self-examination.

As his erection swelled, Broken Blade determinedly pulled the knife from his sheath, folded his breechclout in half and cut across its twelve-inch width. Taking one half of the breechclout, he pulled it up between his legs, grimacing when he discovered how little extra buckskin hung in front or back, and quickly tied the braided leather sash around his waist to hold it in place. His erection caused a portentous bulge in the soft leather.

What remained of his breechclout for Amanda to wear was not nearly long enough to provide much cushioning on horseback but enough to give some protection from the elements, as well as providing a measure of modesty. Therefore, a success, though he felt silly wearing a breechclout only marginally long enough to cover his erection, now nearly fully engorged and throbbing painfully.

It was at this time that Blade realized the fatal flaw in his sartorial plans for his abjectly embarrassed but wildly erotic companion. Though he had a decidedly abbreviated breechclout for Amanda, he didn't have a cord to secure the buckskin in place. After a few frantic seconds, he came to the conclusion that his only option was to take a slice lengthwise from the breechclout to be used as the sash.

A few minutes later he had a finished product. It wasn't much, but something *had* to be better than nothing.

"Turn toward me," Blade said, still on his knees on the bank of the stream.

She turned slowly, and when she saw him on his knees, she seemed surprised.

"I've made a breechclout for you." He held the leather up for her to see.

She caught her lower lip between her teeth and nibbled, an act that, though innocent, was wickedly arousing to Blade's rapidly overheating senses. "I've never . . . I mean . . . um . . . how do you put it on."

"Let me help you," Blade replied, his tone infinitely more casual than his riotous emotions. "Lift the shirt." When she hesitated, he looked up into her troubled gaze. "I'm only trying to help you."

Amanda caught the buckskin shirt at the hips and slowly raised it. Blade watched, hardly breathing, as the leather drifted upward, revealing more and more of the pale thighs, and finally the cleft of her pussy and the triangular patch of dark blonde pubic hair. The feminine vision of beauty completed Blade's erection, which now bulged mightily inside what little remained of his straining buckskin breechclout.

While holding the leather, he reached between Amanda's thighs. Without having to be told, she spread her feet wider apart. Though putting the breechclout in place and securing it with the strip of leather only took a few seconds, they were the most trying seconds of Blade's life.

The spirits are giving me a test. This is punishment for something I have done wrong.

The instant he finished knotting the makeshift sash at Amanda's hip, Blade rose to his feet. She released the buckskin shirt, a faint smile of gratitude touching her full-lipped mouth.

"I can't thank you enough." Something caught her gaze, and she looked down at the enormous length of his erection fighting to be freed from its prison of soft leather. She put a hand to her mouth and whispered through her fingers, "Oh, my! Did I cause that?"

CHAPTER THREE

A hundred distinctly separate emotions went through Amanda in a heartbeat. She thought of her ex-fiancé and how he always said if she got him aroused, then it was her responsibility to see that he was given satisfaction. She didn't see it that way, but to him, that didn't really matter. But she was dutiful, and she did what she was told was her responsibility.

She thought, too, with great bitterness, how when she told Jimmy she was pregnant and that they should move up their wedding date, he had ridden out of town the following morning and never came back. The fact that Amanda miscarried a week later kept the secret of her pregnancy from the town's gossips, but there were still those wagging tongues who speculated on why he had left town so suddenly.

But that was Jimmy, and though he had taught Amanda that making love could be a pleasurable experience, his erection now seemed to Amanda like a miniature version of what Blade possessed.

"Oh," Amanda said softly. She amended it with, "Oh, my."

Blade just stood there as her gaze stayed for long seconds on the angry-looking bulge in the soft buckskin before finally, very slowly, crawling up the dark abdomen and hairless chest corded with muscles . . . and lastly up to Blade's face. He was starkly handsome with high cheekbones, a wide mouth that faintly mocked, and dark eyes that glittered like wet onyx jewels.

He's so beautiful.

It was a wayward thought, one she wished she hadn't had, but once it was there, she couldn't deny its existence. And when the thought *he's dark as sin itself* went through her mind, she flinched. Young women of Amanda's education and social class were never supposed to think of an Indian man as being at all beautiful and certainly not sexually arousing. But what her socially reinforced prejudices yelled at her and what her own body whispered were polar opposites.

Her tongue slipped nervously out between her lips for only a moment before her hand, somehow disembodied, as though it was another woman's hand, trembled as it crossed the small expanse that separated her from Blade.

Why am I doing this?

On a breath-held moment, she caught one end of the braided leather sash at his waist and gave a slow, steady pull. The leather unknotted, and a moment later the straining buckskin fell to the ground and Blade's cock, very long and fiercely rigid, angling upward and visibly pulsing, sprang free.

Blade sighed with relief, and Amanda gasped softly, a hand rising to her mouth.

"Oh ... my ..." she whispered.

A plethora of conflicting emotions were at work within Amanda. The marrow-deep fear she'd experienced when Blue Elk had taken her hostage after killing everyone else on the train was greater than anything she had previously experienced. But then Blue Elk and Dog tied her to the stakes and cut off her clothes, and her fear-level had reached new heights. Worst of all was looking into Blue Elk's eyes as he casually touched her, her body and soul naked and vulnerable in his tepee, listening to his demeaning and vile words.

But Blade represented something else. Something exotic ... and more than just a little dangerous, but in all the right ways erotic ... indefinably sexy ... a taboo temptation ... a promise of fulfillment that Jimmy's caresses hinted at but never really satisfied.

Amanda had never acted so rashly before, at least not when it involved sex. She wasn't what the preachers called 'easy.' Even so, Blade was somehow the embodiment of sex, the epitome of carnal temptation.

Kiss me. Please, kiss me!

Amanda moistened her lips with the tip of her tongue, searching for the courage to put her longings into words just as Blade took a half-step closer. Her heart seemed to seize up in her chest. Though she began to literally tremble from head to toe, she did not take a step back from the tall, powerful man standing so close she could feel the heat and virility of his body in the marrow of her bones.

He raised a large hand, his fingers long and bronzed. When he touched her lightly to smooth an errant lock of hair away from her eye and behind her ear, it seemed as though she had been given the most sensual caress of her life. Her eyelashes batted briefly against cheeks that had become heated with excitement and embarrassment.

The finger that had smoothed the tresses behind her ear eased beneath the heavy fall of her hair until it rested at the base of her neck.

He moistened his lips with his tongue, and it seemed a devilishly erotic thing to do. When he spoke, his voice was deep, low, unmistakably masculine, and ringing clearly with a formal education that Amanda could only speculate at. "You've had a very difficult time of it. If . . . if you don't want me to kiss you, I won't."

Amanda closed her eyes. It was glaringly obvious that she had sexually aroused Blade, and even though she had done that, he was gentlemanly enough to understand she was vulnerable — and didn't want to take advantage of her weakened physical and emotional state.

Amanda whispered, "Please, kiss me." She opened her eyes and looked up into his dark, glittering, jewel-like eyes.

Her limited experience with men made her feel terribly insecure. "I'm not a virgin, but I've never before asked a man to kiss me." She parceled out the truth very carefully. When Jimmy had sex with her, he'd make her say things like 'fuck me' while they were doing it. She wondered if Blade wanted her to speak so coarsely, or if it was just Jimmy who got excited by such words.

Jimmy had taught her all the slang words for body parts and sex acts and continually prodded her to use them, particularly when she was masturbating him. She hadn't liked using the coarse language when she was with Jimmy, but there was something about Blade that pushed her toward temptation and intemperance.

A half-smile toyed with Blade's mouth as he bent toward her. He hesitated a moment, his lips an inch from Amanda's. Impatient and needy, she leaned into him, tilting her head farther back on her shoulders. He slanted his mouth over hers.

With infinite precision, Amanda was aware of all the different tactile sensations evoked by Blade. She tasted his lips, felt the firm, confident pressure of his mouth sealing over hers, moving slowly, almost leisurely, in stark contrast to the enormously swollen and glaringly impatient arousal she had seen. When he pulled her in closer, she felt that erection touch her, its solid length a barrier between their bodies, burning her through the borrowed buckskin shirt.

She had been kissed before, of course, but she had never before responded so quickly nor so completely to a kiss. And when the tip of his slithering tongue touched her lips, she opened her mouth willingly, wantonly hinting that a deeper exploration, a more intimate kiss, would be to her liking. As Blade's tongue slipped between her lips, the tremulous sigh of pleasure that drifted to her ears was unprecedented for Amanda—because the lustful moan of complete sexual surrender was her own.

His hands landed on her shoulders briefly before the broad palms began making their way slowly down her arms. She literally swayed as he kissed her. His tongue danced with hers. When his hands reached her wrists, long, strong fingers curled around them.

By the time he ended that first kiss, she was incapable of denying him anything. Slick, feminine honey lubricated the lips of her pussy. Her clit was erect and tingling, and her cunt ached for Blade's touch.

Amanda looked down just in time to watch him wrap her fingers around the thick, heavily veined shaft of his cock.

"Oh . . . my," she whispered as she felt the heat of Blade's erection seep into her blood stream. It surprised her that he didn't have so much as a single strand of pubic hair.

She discovered that, while holding his swollen cock, she could not touch her fingertips to her thumbs. Nervously clearing her throat, she worked both hands up and down over the length of his cock, and across the surface of her imagination came the question of whether his size was such that taking him into her body would only cause her pain, or if some pleasure might be possible despite his being so extravagantly endowed.

Fear colored her tone when she said, "You're so big that I don't know if I can . . ."

"I know what to do," Blade replied in answer to the half-formed statement, his hands once more on Amanda's shoulders as she stroked him. She suspected he had heard similar trepidation from his lovers many times before. As though reading her mind, he added, "Trust me. I'll make it magical."

As she stroked him, she watched her hands, mesmerized by their movement. She studied their progress with a certain detached objectivity, as though they belonged to someone else. When a pearl of liquid formed at the slitted tip, Amanda resisted the urge to bend over to lick the drop off. The fact that she had even considered doing such a thing surprised her since she'd never before *willingly* performed that intimacy. She had on occasion been wheedled and cajoled and bullied into doing it by Jimmy. He liked thrusting his cock in her mouth, but he did it in such a way that Amanda couldn't imagine ever finding enjoyment in such an act.

At least, not until she had met Blade. He seemed to be the exception to every rule.

Amanda looked up into Blade's eyes again, and he slanted his mouth once more over hers. When he kissed her, she was incapable of coherent, rational thought. As his tongue traced the circumference of her lips and entered her mouth, all she was capable of was feeling. She had been reduced to nothing more than responsive nerve endings by the sensuality conjured by Blade. She was incapable of frigid inhibition or foolish prejudice. She couldn't think.

He caught the bottom of the buckskin shirt and began raising it. She had to release the hold on his erection, and for several seconds, as the shirt was pulled over her head, she had the eerie sensation of drowning or suffocating, of being helpless against a man who could make her feel things more powerfully than she had thought possible.

But then the shirt was over her head and seconds later, when the half-length breechclout fell to the ground at her feet, Amanda stood completely naked — and it wasn't a feeling she was at all comfortable with. She started to cross her arms over her naked breasts, but he caught her once again by the wrists.

"Don't hide," he said, extending her arms outward. "You are so beautiful. You mustn't hide." He leaned down and kissed her on the cheek, then on the neck. "You're much too precious to hide."

Amanda had never before had the word 'precious' used in conjunction with herself, and most certainly never when she was naked. To hear it now, from a man who fascinated her in a thousand different ways, made her nipples tighten and the feminine nectar flow more freely to her pussy. Sharing her passion with Blade, an Indian, was taboo. But the man was irresistible, his charm an unspoken promise of forbidden pleasure, his sensual expertise dispensed with the casual ease of a man who had proven his skill too often already.

He bared his teeth and nipped at the delicate flesh of her throat. Amanda uttered a short, high-pitched gasp, her head spinning, all her thoughts in a chaotic jumble. She tried to pull her wrists from his grasp, but her efforts were easily thwarted. His physical strength was countless times greater than hers. She felt submissive . . . and the awareness of his masculine dominance made the nectar lubricate the entrance to her feminine temple, preparing her for his cock's lusty invasion.

"B-Blade . . . wait . . . I don't think you realize . . ." Amanda began, a small but still rational part of her brain had suddenly found its voice. But then his mouth, warm and moist, captured the crest of her left breast. He drew a firm suction upon her nipple, his cheeks caving inward as his tongue flicked across the throbbing tip. Her protests died in a whimper. "Oh, God! Blade, that's so . . ."

It was the strangest experience for Amanda. It was both fearful and exciting simultaneously — and in equal measures. When she had been tied up by Blue Elk, the helplessness she felt against his greater power — especially with those rawhide cords wrapped around her wrists and ankles — made her feel defiled, even when he wasn't touching her.

With her wrists trapped within Blade's hands, she similarly felt in bondage. But the sensation this gave her, of being utterly overwhelmed by his masculine presence, dominated by his size and strength, did not make her feel defiled. It made her feel small, though she was by any measure a woman of generous dimensions and by comparison to his stark masculinity, distinctly feminine.

Then there was his heritage, which couldn't be ignored. The man was Blade, and he was a Northern Comanche, tall and proud and too damn handsome for her own good. Since Amanda was a proper schoolteacher—a second generation schoolteacher, in fact—and of Swedish-Irish descent, her options in men were limited to Scandinavians and the Irish. Perhaps out of necessity, a suitor of English or Welsh descent might do. But a Northern Comanche? A half-naked savage from the Plains? Not in a thousand years.

Or, perhaps, somewhat less than a thousand years, Amanda thought in a moment of intellectual clarity as Blade kissed his way across the front of her body, moving without haste from one thoroughly tantalized nipple to one that had so far been neglected.

It was worth the wait. By the time Blade finally sucked her right nipple between his lips, Amanda was on the verge of begging for relief. She did not need to sink to such abject levels of carnal surrender because, obviously an aficionado of seduction, Blade knew exactly how to heighten expectation by increasing delay and precisely when to provide the fulfillment that was necessary.

When he used his teeth on her nipple, Amanda's knees buckled. She started to fall, but his arms whipped around her middle in a heartbeat, holding her up as he continued to suckle upon a breast that literally ached with passion. She pushed her fingers into his long, thick, velvety hair, quite intent upon pulling his mouth away from her over-stimulated breast. But once her fingers were entwined in silken hair as black as a raven's wing, they suddenly refused to do the bidding of her better judgment. In fact, her traitorous hands did quite the opposite. Rather than pulling Blade's heated mouth away from her throbbing nipple, she hugged him even closer, pressing his face into the sumptuous mound.

Amanda had been taught to never use the Lord's name in vain, so even under this moment of astonishing stress, this life-lesson remained intact. However, as she felt Blade easing her to the thick cushion of grass at the edges of a clear-running mountain stream, she heard herself whisper for the first time in her life without being forcibly coerced, "Oh, fuck."

Dreamily, as the cool grass touched her naked shoulders and his tantalizing lips traveled from her breast down her stomach, where he tickled her navel with his tongue for maddening seconds before continuing his downward journey, she smiled to hear herself say something so unladylike. With more confidence and less trepidation, she said, "Fuck . . . me."

"Patience, precious . . . patience. I'll take you there." He chuckled lightly and added, "Such language for a lady to use . . . ."

Again, the sibilant endearment that worked as an aphrodisiac. And that confidence of his. Always the confidence, an invisible underscore to words that assured her in delicious ways and to a sensual degree nothing else ever had.

He knows what he's doing. Amanda closed her eyes, giving up the last vestiges of resistance to seduction. But then, almost immediately and like the woman who poisons her own well, she thought, *He's learned to be this good in the arms of a thousand other women.*

The sensually dampening effect of this self-defeating thought did not last long, because hardly had the reality of other women in Blade's life come to mind when his strong hands were at the insides of her naked thighs, spreading them wider apart. An instant later an inquisitive tongue, perhaps even more skilled than the rest of the man, began a slow journey between the passion-inflamed lips of her pussy before circling and caressing her clitoris.

"Fuck!" she cried again.

She felt his mouth on her clitoris, and his tongue. And

when he upped the ante by easing a finger between the lips of her cunt, Amanda wondered whether it was possible to go to heaven without dying first.

When a second long, bronzed finger eased between her labia while his lips and tongue worked with increasing vigor, she considered death and thought that it wouldn't be too high a price to pay to have Blade take her to the end of this road. But this thought was almost immediately dwarfed in significance when a third finger was inserted as he sucked on her clit with the skill of a connoisseur.

With her heels digging into the soft grass of the stream's bank, Amanda gasped "God!" She arched her back, pressing her pussy against Blade's mouth as an orgasm of frightening intensity began.

There were four extremely powerful contractions, a strange pause, and a final fifth spasm. The strong convulsions were immediately followed with another two or three spasms of diminishing strength and intensity. When the last of the contractions shuddered through her body, it was as though every muscle she possessed had suddenly turned to mush. She slumped to the ground. Blade had stilled his frisking tongue and thrusting fingers.

Seconds ticked slowly away as she tried to comprehend what she had just experienced. Finally, still gulping in air, she asked in a breathy whisper, "What the hell was that?"

"That," he said, easing her legs off his broad, naked shoulders and moving upward to settle his naked length atop her, "was a good beginning."

Amanda felt Blade's erection press against her abdomen, the hard length trapped between their bodies. "Really? Just a beginning?" It seemed impossible that there could be more.

He smiled, his long black hair framing his face, his teeth white in the dim light. "You really must learn to trust me."

Then he pushed into her, his unyielding cock forcing

delicate and over-stimulated tissue to spread, but though her mouth opened, no words were emitted.

He was wrong!

A flash of bitterness swept through her as her body was forced to expand farther than it ever had before and a stiletto blade of pain stabbed through her body, emanating outward from an overheated vagina overstretched by an oversized man.

Blade's initial invasion was partial, hardly more than a quarter of his length. Though inexperienced in such matters, and even though her teeth were clenched against the pain, she was aware that her lover had not cruelly bore into her. He knew his size just as he understood her limitations, and for that, Amanda wrapped her arms more tightly around his neck and breathed, "Thank you."

As he withdrew, she felt a sense of relief . . . and nascent pleasure hinted at something significantly more evocative. For breath-held seconds, he withdrew slowly until only the very tip of his crown still separated the lips of her pussy. He hesitated, waiting, his patience infinite when hers was not. Her fingernails gouged into the flesh of his taut buttocks, prompting a downward thrust that filled her completely, even though he had not given her all he possessed.

"Oh, God!" she gasped, feeling herself swell, expanding to accommodate, opening to his relentless thrust.

But even on the second thrust, he did not give her everything he had. It wasn't until the third revolution of Blade's lean hips that Amanda at last felt his torso pressing against hers, his erection deeply buried within her . . . and she knew at last that she had taken all that this dangerous man had to give.

"Oh, yes!" she whispered, holding Blade tightly, her legs looped around his thighs. "Just wait . . . Just give me a second . . . You're just so . . ." A shudder went through her. She held him a little more tightly. "Big."

Once again, treasonously, the notion slithered through her consciousness that she was not the first woman to have some difficulty adjusting to Blade's dimensions and requested tolerance and self-discipline on his part lest intended ecstasy become agony.

Amanda cursed herself for the thought. She knew she had no right to make a claim on his past.

"Let me know," Blade said, his breath warm against the side of her face, his lean body tense from head to toe.

Holding his body tightly to her own, his powerful chest pressing against the full mounds of her breasts, Amanda was struck with the image of Blade being a thoroughbred at the racetrack, quivering with anticipation in preparation for the opening of the gates and the beginning of the race. It seemed to her that making love was what he was born and bred to do.

"You're just so . . ."

Her words faded when he began a slow retreat, the unyielding shaft pulling at her tender labia and rubbing so near an aroused clitoris. With just the tip of his cock still between the lips of her pussy, he hesitated, waiting. Her cheek was pressed against his when she nodded, and this time the invasion was faster, impaling her with his entire erection. This time he gave her everything he had.

As his torso slapped against hers, she whispered, "Yesss."

Like a locomotive engine steadily being given more coal for the fire, Blade began slowly. But each thrust, each invasion followed by retreat, happened just a little more quickly than the previous one. Amanda came a second time, her body twitching beneath Blade's, his hips churning as he filled her with his lust-hardened flesh. She had never before had an orgasm while her lover's erection was filling her, so when the spasms started, she accepted them with an almost grateful sense of wonder. Discordantly, she thought it curious that an uncivilized heathen warrior such as Blade should be the man to expand her worldview so thoroughly.

Amanda felt his breath burning the side of her face, heard the hoarse gasps of his labor as he pummeled her body, no longer the practiced lover with a velvety touch, now a virile warrior stripped down to his primordial elements. She was wondering if yet a third orgasm was possible when he suddenly withdrew completely. An instant later, he groaned deep in his chest, and she felt the thick, heated eruptions of his climax hit her stomach.

Stroking his hair, holding him close, his erection trapped between their bodies and his semen warm and slippery against her skin, she whispered, "Thank you . . . thank you for everything, but especially for not climaxing inside me."

Blade put his weight on his elbows, lifting up enough so that he could look into Amanda's eyes. "Precious, that was exquisite." He smiled and kissed the tip of her nose, the point of her chin, then her mouth. "And now I think we both could use a quick dip in the stream."

"In a second," she said, pulling him back down so that his chest again pressed against the mounds of her breasts. Even though he was a big man, Amanda was in no hurry at all to have his weight off her. "In a second."

Amanda was drifting tranquilly in the half-world between sleep and consciousness. She was on her side, her head resting on the biceps of Blade's left arm. Through the buckskin shirt, she felt the heat of his chest against her back and the front of his naked thighs against the backs of hers, his pelvis against her bottom. She did not want to wake up. Bliss was right here in her semi-conscious dream world, and bliss was an emotional state she had experienced too few times in her life.

She heard and felt Blade yawn, and a sleepy smile curled

her full-lipped mouth. Blade was awake. Amanda remembered feeling him get up several times during the night to check the surrounding area to make sure that they were still safe. Then he would come back to her, his body large and warm as he slid up against her, easing one arm beneath her head as his other hand went around her body to rest against her stomach, touching her lightly but possessively through the buckskin shirt.

She was aware of the morning sun against her face, and though she wanted nothing more than to remain in Blade's arms, she blinked her eyes several times, but then closed them again.

"Good morning." Blade's voice was low, a soft purr of sound. "I wondered when you would wake up."

"I'm not awake." Amanda didn't try to hide the impishness of her smile. "I'm sleeping very peacefully, thank you very much."

His body moved as he chuckled silently. In her muzzy-minded state, it seemed that she was surrounded and protected by his powerful, warrior's body.

Blade took his hand from Amanda's stomach and, with his forefinger, smoothed hair away from her temple. A little shiver went through her when his fingertip lightly touched her face. For a moment, she held her breath, still not entirely awake yet distinctly aware of all the places where her body was in contact with his.

He traced the circumference of her ear. As she came slowly to full consciousness, she was aware of her own awakening passion. The surface of her skin tingled, and her clitoris began to itch pleasingly. A sensual warmth spread slowly outward from her pussy.

"You're beautiful when you sleep."

His voice caressed her intimately. She felt it as surely as she felt his fingertip sliding along her eyebrow, her cheek, her temple, her ear. When Blade's rapidly swelling penis pressed against her bottom, she parted her thighs just enough to allow his erection to slip between her legs.

"Blade . . . ."

The single word came from her as a breathy sigh. He moved his hips forward, his erection continuing to grow, sliding against the moistening lips of her pussy.

"So beautiful." Blade eased his left arm out from beneath her head.

Amanda kept her eyes closed as she surrendered the control of her body over to Blade, her feminine instincts whispering that she wanted to go wherever he wanted to take her. She was willingly submissive to his dominating presence and spirit.

He rolled her slowly onto her stomach, and she cradled her head in her arms as he lifted her hips and pushed the buckskin shirt up to the small of her back to expose the pale curves of her ass. A moment later, when the bulbous crown of his erection rubbed up and down over the lips of her cunt, which had already become slick and creamy with her excitement, Amanda merely sighed her acquiescence.

He eased into her slowly, the shaft of his cock thick, unyielding. A warbling whimper came from her as he filled her tight channel.

"You make me wet . . . so fast," she whispered once he'd reached full insertion.

She wanted to ask how he could excite her so thoroughly, so quickly and easily, but he began moving his hips, working the length of his cock in and out of her pussy, and the sensations elicited from each invasion and retreat were of such an intensity that she no longer wished to *know*, only to *feel*.

Sometime later, it would occur to Amanda that beginning the day with a bone-melting climax put something of a golden glow to the rest of the morning, and well into the afternoon.

"How much farther is it to your camp?" Amanda asked, her cheek against Blade's shoulder as she rode behind him on Tikki. The lovemaking that morning had been even more glorious than the previous evening, and she was feeling spectacularly lazy.

"If you had a horse of your own, it would be two days. With Tikki having to carry both of us, it'll take twice that long."

Amanda smiled, inhaled deeply, then sighed with contentment. Four days with Blade? The way she felt right now, she wouldn't mind if the trip took a month. Or three.

They rode in silence for a long time before he asked, "I would imagine you're anxious to get back to your world."

"My world?"

"The civilized world."

"Trust me, it's not that civilized." She remembered the look in Jimmy's eyes when she said she was pregnant, and they'd have to push their wedding date forward. In his eyes was contempt for her. He had quietly disappeared from town by the next morning. "The clothes are different, and I suppose we do certain things differently, but it isn't a more civilized world. It's just different."

"While we're in camp, I'm responsible for you," Blade said.

Amanda grinned sleepily. Discovering that Blade was responsible for her added an unexpected touch of eroticism to the awareness.

"You were headed to Colorado City, right?"

She nodded, her head against the back of his shoulder.

"Don't worry. I'll see that you get there as soon as possible."

She leaned away from him. She wasn't in any hurry to part company from Blade, but it seemed as though he had already made a schedule for getting rid of her.

Aware now that her time with him most definitely was limited, she put her cheek against his shoulder again and not knowing what else to say and certainly not meaning it honestly, whispered, "Thank you."

CHAPTER FOUR

When they reached the encampment, there wasn't a soul in the tribe who wasn't waiting to greet Blade, and speculate on the woman riding double on his pinto and wearing a buckskin shirt but not much else.

"You're sure they're not going to be angry you've brought me along?" Amanda felt very vulnerable and completely underdressed while being scrutinized by countless pairs of dark eyes.

"You're with me," Blade replied, as though that somehow answered all of her questions. He dropped his left hand down to her naked thigh.

"Please, people are watching," Amanda said, though she did not push his hand from her leg.

"You'll have to get used to our ways. The Northern Comanche aren't as hypocritical as men and women in your white world." He glanced over his shoulder, and she was reminded once again of his exotic, dark beauty. "Wait 'til you meet my mother. You'll love her. Everyone does."

The word 'mother' sent a frisson of excitement through her. He had seemed so bold, so utterly masculine, it never occurred to her that he would have the feminine influence of a mother in his life. But the pride in his tone, the undisguised love, made her all the more curious to meet his family, to discover how he had become the man that he was.

"Does she speak English?" Amanda instantly wanted to know everything about his youth, about what he had been like as a little boy. It never occurred to her that asking such a question might be interpreted as insulting.

"Of course she does," Blade said after a moment. "She's as white as you are. In fact, she's from England."

Amanda caught the coloring of disapproval in Blade's tone and made a promise to herself to think through her questions in the future before putting them into words.

She guessed there were well over one hundred tepees in the encampment. She noticed, too, that more than a few young women were looking at Blade with covetous eyes. When they looked at her, their expressions universally changed to emotions varying from mild disapproval to outright scorn.

The women adore Blade, Amanda thought.

Amanda felt a growing resentment at the fawning attention her lover received. Women reached up to touch him as they rode Tikki through camp.

I wouldn't be surprised if he has a dozen young women vying for his attention.

The thought that he might have a wife filtered through her mind, and she squeezed her eyes shut for a moment, mentally forcing the notion away. She wondered how much of the contempt she saw in the young squaws was because she was with Blade, or if it was because she was white.

A man wearing an elaborately beaded buckskin shirt, with similarly beaded leggings and moccasins, stepped into the path of Blade's pinto.

"Welcome home, my son," the man said, his dark face almost glowing with pleasure and pride. "Were you successful?"

Blade replied, "Blue Elk is dead."

"Good. And the woman?"

"Blue Elk and his men attacked a train. They killed everyone and took her."

"You saved the woman's life." It was a statement, not a

question. He appeared pleased with Blade's actions. "I'll bet you're hungry. Come, the women have been preparing a feast for you since the sentries spotted you at Connor's Bluff."

Blade flashed a smile at his father before looking over his shoulder at Amanda. "We rode past Connor's Bluff about three hours back. I'm afraid I have some business to attend to with my father, but the women will see to it you have everything you need."

Blade's mother, Constance, was the very essence of courtesy. She had dark blonde hair with sparkling green eyes that were clear and bright. She was a little taller than Amanda, and her body was becoming plumper the nearer to fifty she got. Constance's diction was flawlessly British, in startling contrast to the visual image given by her beaded and fringed buckskin dress and moccasins.

Constance inquired politely about Amanda's ordeal but was careful to not pry. Knowing she had to have an explanation for wearing Blade's buckskin shirt, and though the women gathered in Constance's tepee had not inquired, Amanda explained in matter-of-fact terms that Blue Elk had intended on raping her and would have done the deed had she not been rescued.

"Your son saved my life," she said to Constance. "I'll never be able to repay him."

A mother's proud smile spread across Constance's face. "That's my son," she said with a pronounced British accent. She then turned her attention to a very attractive young squaw still in her teens. "Moon Will Shine, please get some dresses for our guest to wear."

At hearing the request, Moon's gaze flashed over to Amanda. Behind the dark glance was anger, though Moon allowed it to show for only a moment. Still, Amanda had caught the resentment, and she suspected she had an enemy within the tribe that would not be easily placated. Moon left the tepee a moment later, without saying a word.

That left Amanda with Constance and three elderly women. "I don't think she likes me very much."

"Moon is the widow of Blade's brother," Constance explained. For a moment, grief was etched in her countenance.

"Widow? She seems so young."

"She's just nineteen winters," Constance said. "For a woman of the Northern Comanche, sixteen winters is when she takes a husband."

"What is it for men?"

"Twenty-five winters." Constance smiled. "A man must be a complete man before he can take on the responsibility of caring for wives and children. Besides, girls mature more quickly than boys."

"How did Blade's brother die?" Amanda asked and immediately regretted the question when sadness teared up in Constance's eyes. "I'm sorry. I shouldn't have asked. It's just that I'm so curious about Blade — well, about all of you, I guess."

Constance shook her head and made a motion with her hand as though to dismiss Amanda's concern. "Blade's brother, Kills With Knives, was attacked by a Kiowa war party late last winter. The Kiowa and the Northern Comanche have been at war with each other for generations. Sometimes there's an effort at a truce, but it never lasts long. There's too much bad blood, too much animosity between us for a truce to last."

She spoke with a weariness that startled Amanda. She suddenly had the appearance of an attractive, middle-aged woman who had personally been at war for a hundred years, and the change was a shockingly abrupt departure from the bright-eyed woman who had taken such pleasure in discussing her son's adventures.

"I'm sorry," Amanda said.

She was about to say more, but Moon stepped in through the tepee entrance with an armful of dresses and moccasins. Her dark eyes were chilly as she placed the garments on the buffalo mat beside Amanda.

"Now, take off my son's shirt, and let's find a dress that's presentable," Constance said, moving closer to inspect the clothing that had been brought.

Amanda pulled the buckskin shirt over her head. Moon made a derisive, snorting sound, her mouth twisting unpleasantly. The elderly women, who didn't speak a word of English, exchanged glances. All Amanda was certain of was that she had done something wrong, something she should probably be embarrassed about.

"What is it? What have I done?" Amanda resisted the urge to hide her body with her hands.

Constance again made a dismissive, waving motion with her hands. "I'll explain that later. For now, try on this."

She handed over a doeskin dress of the softest leather Amanda had ever felt. The sleeveless dress was essentially two pieces of leather sewn together, with beadwork depicting a buffalo hunt on the front. She pulled the dress over her head and stood so that it hung on her body properly.

"It's too tight across the bosom," Constance noted. "But the rest seems fine."

"I should lose weight."

"Nonsense. Our braves like their squaws to look like women." Constance inspected the stitching on the dress's shoulder and beneath the arm. "Among the men here, a skinny wife or child is considered a sign that the husband cannot provide sufficiently for his family."

I'm not Blade's wife.

Amanda soon realized it was much easier having thoughts of Blade being a husband than it was in banishing such romantic thoughts. Once Constance had broached the subject, whenever there was the slightest lull in the conversation,

Amanda's thoughts drifted to idyllic, highly romanticized notions of sharing her life with the tall, gorgeous warrior who had recently taught her what pleasures were possible when in the arms of a man.

Constance turned to the elderly women and spoke in a language Amanda didn't understand. She was then told to remove the dress, and moments after that, the women and Moon left the tepee. Amanda was given a buffalo robe to cover her nudity.

"We're alone now," Amanda said. "Why did Moon snicker so condescendingly at me?"

"You have body hair." Constance smiled and blushed a little. "I remember when I fell in love and came here to live with his people. I thought it was strange, too. The customs of the Northern Comanche are not just rooted in mysticism and religion. Some customs are absolute necessities if the tribe is to flourish. Other customs, I suppose, are followed simply because they've always been followed, and nobody questions their meaning or origin."

"Why would they get rid of their body hair?" Amanda recalled being surprised when she saw that Blade didn't have a single strand of pubic hair. And when she had been captive, Blue Elk had tugged hard enough on her pubic hair to remove several strands.

"Like most of the tribes of the Plains, the Northern Comanche believe that the hair on their head is intractably connected to their soul. From the moment they begin growing body hair, they remove it so that the only hair their soul will be connected to is the hair on their head." She shrugged. "If you keep plucking the hairs, it doesn't take long for the hair to stop growing altogether."

Amanda had never before heard such a thing, and the surprise showed in her expression.

"We used to use clamshells and pinched them together to

remove the hairs, but we do a great deal of trading with the settlers, so now we use tweezers." She picked up a gourd and took a sip of the liquid inside, then handed over the gourd to Amanda. "Having body hair is considered unhygienic to the Northern Comanche. That's why Moon looked so disgusted." Her gaze met Amanda's, and the wife of the tribe's chief asked, "How long would you like to stay with us?"

The frankness and unexpectedness of the question caught Amanda completely off guard. After several seconds of silence, she finally replied, "I . . . I'm not sure, really. Is it a bother to have me here?"

Constance's smile was enigmatic. "By the way, since Blade is your protector, you'll be staying in his tent."

There were nearly one thousand men, women, and children of the Northern Comanche tribe headed by Parker Two Shoes, and nearly all of them were involved in the raucous celebration thrown to honor the safe return of Broken Blade after his mission of vengeance upon Blue Elk.

"The woman—she's important to you?"

Blade turned and looked down at his father. Blade towered over Parker, thanks to the genes passed down from his maternal grandfather, who was well over six feet tall.

"Yes," he said after giving the question some consideration. "I didn't really expect it to happen."

Parker chuckled softly. "I didn't expect to fall in love with a white woman, either. But then I looked into your mother's green eyes and all those great convictions I had about marrying within the tribe disappeared like smoke." He smiled at the memory. "I've never regretted my decision. Not for an hour, a minute, or even a second."

Moon Will Shine stepped closer, holding a pottery bowl in both hands. Inside the bowl was a man-sized portion of stew.

The stew—a concoction of water, buffalo meat, potatoes, and any greens or vegetables that could be found—was the staple diet of the Northern Comanche.

Blade smiled at his older brother's widow. In the language of the Comanche, a dialect of the Shoshonean family, he thanked the young widow. As he took the bowl from her, Moon's fingers drifted along the backs of his hands considerably longer than necessary. He took the spoon from her, nodded his approval of her gift of food, then turned back to his father. Moon, understanding and accepting the protocol of the tribe that put warriors on a different level from squaws, walked away . . . but not before she glanced back over her shoulder, her eyes glittering like jewels with open coquetry.

"I'll never be able to finish all of this," Blade said as he put a spoon into the bowl. "Mom's been feeding me constantly since I got back."

Parker was the highest-ranking political leader of the Northern Comanche, and he had never been a man given to small-talk, so Blade wasn't particularly taken aback when his father asked bluntly, "Are you going to take Moon Will Shine as a wife?"

Blade looked at his father for a moment before replying. "I thought she was in mourning."

"Her period of mourning ended with the full moon. As your brother's eldest male sibling, you are responsible for her."

Blade hadn't known Moon's period of honoring her husband's life and mourning his death had passed. It hadn't seemed like that much time had passed since the murder. Almost on a daily basis, Blade thought about his beloved older brother, remembering all the magnificent times they'd had together, all the shared memories. He didn't have to be told that custom dictated Moon was his responsibility, and it irked him that his father had put his duties to the tribe into words.

"What about the white squaw?" Parker asked.

Blade smiled. "She's not a squaw, and you know that."

"If you take her as your wife, she'll be considered a squaw." Parker shrugged his shoulders. "I took a yellow eyes for a wife, and it was the smartest decision I've ever made. But that was long ago, and I didn't have a brother's widow to think about." He smiled and placed a hand on Blade's shoulder. "Moon's awfully easy on the eyes, she's a wonderful cook, an excellent seamstress, and she adores the ground you walk on. You could do a lot worse than have Moon as one of your wives."

"I know that." Blade wished his father would drop the subject of his bachelorhood. "She stays in my tepee. I'll see she has plenty to eat, that she'll want for nothing."

"Look into her eyes sometime," Parker said, giving his son's shoulder a squeeze. "She wants more from you than to see that she's got food to eat, hides to make warm clothes with for the winter, and security. She wants a husband . . . in her bed."

Amanda told herself she wasn't going to get jealous. She told herself that her time with Blade was limited and that he had made it quite clear he would make sure she made it to Colorado City quickly, so she obviously had no claim on him—at least none that he might recognize. So. it was all really quite simple. She just wouldn't get envious.

It didn't work, though not for lack of trying.

There were no less than a dozen young, pretty women flittering around Blade at all times during the celebration. The women—girls, really—were, without variation, slender and attired in buckskin dresses elaborately adorned with quillwork and beads. It was impossible to not notice all the ladies were wearing their finest dresses. Without exception, the women had long hair, some all the way to their waist, parted down the middle and festooned with owl, eagle, and hawk feathers, and ribbons of various colors.

Constance approached Amanda and touched her forearm before speaking. "Have you had enough to eat?"

"More than enough. Thank you." She gave Constance a smile but couldn't resist glancing quickly back at Blade. There seemed to be fewer coquettish ladies vying for his attention now. There couldn't be more than eight or nine stunning young women smiling flirtatiously at him. "Blade seems to be quite the hero."

Constance looked at her son. "The tribal elders are unhappy that he hasn't taken a wife yet. The young women — they all know his time is running out. His days as a bachelor are numbered."

The words cut into Amanda's heart. Memories as precise as reality flooded her senses. She remembered the weight and feel of Blade's powerful body above her, crushing her to the grass as his beautiful cock pumped deep and hard into her receptive body. It was as though she could once again feel his long-fingered hands caressing her, stroking her flesh to ignite fires of lust that swept away her inhibitions. It all came back to her like a tidal wave, and for a moment, green-eyed jealousy flashed through her heart.

"Well, it's obvious that he'll have quite a number of women to choose from." The words came out clipped and bitter.

Constance smiled and touched Amanda's forearm. "Why don't you go over there and talk to him? He's quite an accomplished conversationalist."

Oh, Constance, your son is accomplished at much more than just conversation.

CHAPTER FIVE

Blade found Amanda at the very outskirts of the camp, standing by herself, looking up at the stars. For a moment, he just looked at her from a distance. The beauty of her curvaceous body and the delicacy of her facial features insinuated itself into his masculine appreciation. A smile touched his lips. Most Northern Comanche squaws weren't nearly as voluptuous as Amanda, and he suddenly found himself favoring her more dramatic form of feminine allure.

As though sensing his presence, she suddenly looked at him. She did not smile. That, he knew, wasn't a good sign.

"Not enjoying the celebration?" he asked, stepping closer.

"It's not that I'm not enjoying myself," she said with little inflection in her voice. "I just got tired of watching all those beautiful women touching you constantly."

A smile tugged at Blade's mouth. He was accustomed to being touched by women, just as he was familiar with jealous flareups between his lovers. What he wasn't accustomed to was seeing Amanda, in all her blonde Nordic glory, wearing a lavishly ornamented Northern Comanche ceremonial dress. He liked her appearance in the traditional clothing of his tribe. He also appreciated the fact that she was both jealous and possessive of him, and this was monumentally surprising. Never before in his life had he tolerated a lover to openly display either of those traits, and he wondered now, why they were acceptable from Amanda.

As he stepped up to touch her arm, he said, "They meant no harm."

She flinched and took a step away. "Your mother is quite a woman."

Even in the dim light, he saw the anger flash in Amanda's green eyes. "Yes, she is." It seemed a safe thing to say, but once the words were out of his mouth, he wasn't so sure.

"She told me that you're supposed to be picking a bride soon." Her mouth twisted in a way that didn't favor her beauty. "Just one bride, or were you planning on having a harem?"

Blade now understood Amanda's anger, but his own anger piqued at hearing the condescension in her tone. He had lived his life without answering to any woman, and he wasn't inclined to start now. "There are certain advantages all around for a warrior to have more than one wife." It was an honest, if incomplete, answer.

Amanda snorted derisively. "I can imagine what the advantages are."

"If a warrior has two wives, it cuts the work they must do in half. If he has three wives, then the work is divided even more." He again stepped closer, and though Amanda flinched when he put his hand on her shoulder, she didn't step away this time. "But for what it's worth, I can't really see any man needing more than you." He smiled boyishly, but his tone was low and husky when he added, "You're more than a handful as it is."

Not in the least bit mollified, Amanda asked, "Is that supposed to make me feel better? Or maybe you're saying something about my figure?"

She turned away, folding her arms beneath her breasts. Blade doubted the move had been intended to be erotic, but with her arms folded together, they pushed her breasts upward, displaying more of their creamy bounty above the U-shaped neckline of her doeskin dress.

And since all Northern Comanche women are expected to

be able to ride, the two halves of women's dresses were not stitched below the hip to allow straddling a pony. It had not been Amanda's intention to give him a view of her thigh almost to the curve of her bottom, but that's what she did. And as the tall war chief of the Northern Comanche looked at her, his cock—always alert to feminine charms, especially Amanda's—awoke from its light slumber and began to respond.

"You're beautiful." Blade took Amanda by the shoulder and turned her so that she faced him.

He had turned her so he couldn't see her thigh and wouldn't think about how carnally exquisite it was to have her legs surrounding his lean hips as he thrust his cock into her. But by turning Amanda around, he was now given a view of her bountiful breasts. Her cleavage drew his eyes magnetically, and vague but scintillating questions tickled his curiosity as he considered what pleasures he would experience when sliding his erection between her breasts.

The mental, visual imagine of looking down and seeing as well as feeling his erection sliding between her breasts was so power if actually made a shiver go through him.

Blade's cock, now fully awake, was very quickly outgrowing the confines of the elaborately beaded and fringed ceremonial breechclout that hung to his knees. It seemed whenever Amanda was within touching distance, his libido was always aroused, his body needing only the slightest hint of appreciation to respond approvingly.

"Let's not argue," he said, gently massaging her upper arms.

When she tilted her face up to his, the breath caught in his throat. Her face, shining in the light, was a vision of such ethereal splendor that for a moment, he wondered if he was really looking at the woman he had rescued from Blue Elk's tepee or if she wasn't a vision conjured up by the spirits to haunt his peace of mind.

The spirits were usually kind to Blade — they had been kind all his life — having blessed him with looks, charm, stature, strength, and an indefatigability that was legendary. Still, it wasn't good to question the benevolence of the spirits.

He touched her cheek lightly with his fingertips to make sure she wasn't just a spirit's specter.

"Sometimes you look at me with the strangest expression on your face," she said quietly. "I never know what's going on in that brain of yours."

He passed the pad of his thumb lightly over her lips. Her eyes closed for a moment, and she appeared even more spectral and erotic in the dappled light.

In a whisper that barely reached Blade's ears, she said, "When you touch me, I melt inside. I keep telling myself I shouldn't be so responsive to you. I really do. But it doesn't do any good." Her eyes opened, and she looked up at him with an expression of helpless passion. "Do me a favor and don't let me know which women in camp you've slept with. I don't want to know who your lovers are — past, present, or future." Then, so softly that he had to bend to hear her words on the night breeze, she added, "We both know I've got no claim on you, but that doesn't stop me from pretending."

Blade kept Amanda from saying any more by slanting his mouth over hers. She slipped her arms around his middle, and as his tongue eased between her lips, he was stricken with the awareness that this voluptuous yellow eyes with golden hair fit perfectly to his body. He pulled her in more tightly, the sensation of her heavy breasts compressing against his chest thrilled his senses like a narcotic flowing straight into his veins to make his head swim.

Her lips parted in invitation. He eased his tongue between their soft fullness, tasting her sweetness. Her tongue greeted his, moving erotically, allowing him to explore more deeply.

As he kissed her, his hands slid over soft doeskin until he cupped the rounded cheeks of her ass. He swallowed the sigh she emitted and pulled her in so that she had no choice but to feel how he sexually responded to her.

Without ever stopping his kiss, his hands moved to her hips, eased between the two halves of her dress, then slid inward again. This time his long-fingered hands cupped her naked bottom, and the warmth and smoothness of her skin added the last necessary inducements for his erection to reach maximum size.

Amanda lifted her arms, entwined them around his neck, and turned her face aside to end the kiss. In a whisper, she said, "Now I know why the Northern Comanche don't wear bloomers. It's to make loving convenient for randy warriors like you."

Blade smiled, his hands moving lightly over the twin mounds of her ass. "Actually, it's because we haven't much cloth, but that's going to get remedied soon enough." He moved his hips just enough to rub the swollen length of his cock against her stomach. "But I'll admit there are advantages to you not having bloomers."

Despite the softness of the buckskin breechclout, the size of his erect cock made wearing *any* clothing uncomfortable. Scintillating memories tickled his senses of what it had felt like to push through Amanda's resistance for the very first time, feeling the slick, pink lips of her pussy expanding as his hard cock invaded deeper and deeper until at last, he was fully embedded, and their bodies were intimately joined.

"Advantages that both of us are currently enjoying," she purred, rolling her head on her shoulders, clearly savoring his caresses.

"Not angry anymore?"

"I should be furious with you for letting all those simpering girls fawn all over you," Amanda replied, tension in the corners of her eyes. "You saved my life, and you taught me what real passion feels like. I know I shouldn't be nasty and jealous, and the day is going to come when I'll have to leave to go back to my world. I just don't want to think about that right now." She sighed and nibbled thoughtfully on her lower lip for a moment. "So, what about what your mother said? How many wives are you going to choose?"

He squeezed her ass with both hands. "Let's not talk about that now."

Amanda flinched. He flinched, too. He hadn't intended on implying any kind of permanence with her. The differences between them were enormous, and he had the gold mine and the acquisition of land to concentrate on.

He had seen with his own eyes the avaricious greed of the yellow eyes. Treaties and agreements meant nothing when gold was involved. He had been taught by his father and grandfather that the only hope for the Northern Comanche lay in having deeds to land that couldn't be voided in court and gold in the bank that couldn't be stolen. Land and money were the weapons that would protect the tribe, and to that end, Blade couldn't let anything, or anyone, change his focus.

The sound of young squaws giggling drew his attention, and he found himself looking at several teenage girls, each smiling with naughty delight at having caught the tribe's war chief in a compromising position. He instantly took his hands from Amanda's naked bottom and spun to face them.

"You've had your laugh," he said in his native tongue, unable to keep the smile from his face. "Run along and pester some boys your own age."

With a chorus of giggles, the girls hurried away, chattering busily among themselves.

Turning back to Amanda, he said, "I'd better make an appearance, but it shouldn't take me long. Go back to my tepee and wait for me there."

Blade was surprised that, for once, Amanda didn't have a snappy rebuttal to his telling her what to do. He watched her walk away, then looked down and adjusted the front flap of his breechclout so the whole tribe wouldn't know just how enticing he found the golden-haired woman who seemed to be the topic of countless conversations in camp.

Amanda's moccasin-shod feet seemed to barely touch the ground as she walked to Blade's tepee. She hadn't given much serious consideration to being Blade's wife. Their differences were monumental. And, being honest with herself, she admitted that while she was beginning to learn quite a bit about Blade and his family, his tribe, and the things that were important to him, he knew almost nothing about her or the world she lived in.

As she walked, oblivious to the carnival-like chaos going on all around her, she considered what the ramifications would be if she should take Blade into her world. It only took a moment for Amanda to conclude that her world would be far less willing to admit an outsider into their ranks than his tribe was in making her feel welcome.

Amanda wondered if she could even go back to Twin Crossings, back to the school where she taught, doing her level best to teach children to read and write, always wondering when their parents would pull them out of school so that the youngsters could spend their days working on the farm.

She reached Blade's tepee. The entrance flap was pulled aside, held in place by a slender cord. She loosened the cord and, bending low to enter, let the leather flap fall into place, giving her privacy.

Inside, it was extremely dark, with the only illumination being the moonlight filtering in through the smoke hole at the top of the tepee. There were two beds made of buffalo hides and wool blankets, the latter obviously purchased from white traders. She considered which bed to take, feeling utterly without morals because in minutes or maybe even seconds, Blade would return and make love to her. Possibly for hours. Maybe even days.

She slipped out of her moccasins, then pulled the doeskin dress over her head and tossed it aside. Completely naked, Amanda paused a moment, closing her eyes, thinking about Blade. As though moving by magic, her right hand slipped down low, sensitive fingertips trailing lightly over her abdomen and past soft pubic curls before skipping feather-soft over tingling labia. Hazy images of the nights of passion she'd shared with Blade during their ride back to the encampment drifted over the surface of her mind.

"Ohhh," she sighed aloud, the pad of her middle finger instantly finding her clitoris. She knew just exactly how to touch herself to provide the maximum amount of pleasure.

She knew from experience.

She rolled her head on her shoulders as she pleasured herself, her right hand tantalizing her pussy while she pinched and tugged on her nipples with her left. In her mind's eye she saw Blade, his chest naked and sweaty, the muscles of his pectorals crisply defined, the ripples of hard abdomen muscles practically begging to be traced by her tongue.

Opening her eyes at last, she stopped caressing herself. She once more looked at the two beds and decided the bigger of the two would be Blade's. She considered waiting for him atop the bed, completely naked and ready for his loving, but that was a bit too bold for her. Instead, she slipped beneath the light blanket, her eyes on the low entrance to the tepee as she waited for the man who had taught her just what ecstasy a woman's body was capable of experiencing.

When Blade stepped into his tepee a moment later, whatever insecurities Amanda harbored, vanished. Despite all the beautiful, young, slender squaws he had his choice of later, he wanted her now and with a sensual greediness that made her pussy tingle.

She felt coveted, and it was a feeling she liked.

"I got here as quickly as I could," he explained, standing near the center of the tepee. He pulled his ornate buckskin war shirt over his head, and when she saw his naked torso, the breath caught in her throat. Not until she had met Blade had she ever really considered a man's body to be arousing to look at.

Dressed only in his long breechclout and moccasins, all dark-skinned perfection and lean-muscled beauty, he appeared wild, untamed, uncivilized—a man at the absolute pinnacle of masculine splendor. When he kicked out of his moccasins, then unknotted the braided leather sash so that his breechclout fell away, exposing a half-formed arousal, she moaned low in her throat.

He started to get down on the buffalo hide bed with her, but she quickly put a hand up to stop him. "Wait. Just . . . just stand there a moment," she said, her voice hushed with the lustful tension that gripped her soul. "I want to look at you."

The right side of his mouth quirked upward in a smile. Completely naked and supremely confident, he stood up straight and put his hands on his hips. Rolling so that she was on her back beneath the light blanket, Amanda raised her knees a little, then touched her pussy intimately. Her lashes batted against her cheeks briefly before she forced her eyes open wide.

"You're so beautiful," she whispered. "Can I ask a favor of you?"

His brows rose. "Why not?"

"Would you touch yourself?"

Amanda heard the request and knew she was the one who had spoken it, yet the words seemed utterly foreign to her.

Amanda Murchison simply wasn't the type of woman who asked such things of men. That's what she tried to tell herself, anyway.

Blade took his cock in his hand and moved his fist back and forth. Within seconds, his arousal grew to its full, formidable length and girth. As he stroked himself into a state of iron-hard rigidity, Amanda eased a single finger between the moist, tingling lips of her pussy. She was very wet, so much so that the penetration of a single finger was almost friction-free.

"How is it," she asked, her voice quavering slightly as her senses rapidly heated, "that whenever I'm with you, I find myself wanting to do the wickedest things?"

Blade shrugged. As he brought his fist back and forth over his cock, the muscles in his chest rippled and slid beneath the bronzed skin. She felt an overpowering urge to suck on his nipples and taste the tang of fresh perspiration on his skin.

A drop of fluid formed at the tip of his cock, the nectar glistening like a precious pearl in the dim moonlight. Her labia swelled in anticipation. Her middle finger eased between well-lubricated folds, gliding smoothly over her erect clitoris.

"Let me see your . . . ." Amanda's words faltered until she decided on " . . . it." Amanda's tone suggested she would beg, if necessary, to have her wishes fulfilled.

Blade released his cock. Its great length stood out from his body, angling slightly upward, the head and shaft enormously swollen with desire. Her pupils dilated at the vision of virile, masculine perfection. His erection appeared overtly dangerous, yet its attraction was undeniable. As she stared at his cock, her right hand beat faster between spread thighs, pumping a single finger in and out of her pussy.

When he spoke, his deep voice was like a caress to her senses. "Get rid of the blanket," he said, his hands at his hips, his enormous shaft jutting out prominently. "I want to watch you, too."

"I feel so naughty when I'm with you," Amanda replied without any censure.

She tossed the blanket aside, spread her knees even wider apart, and began using the fingertips of her left hand on her clitoris as she pumped a single finger from her right hand between the delicate, pink lips of her pussy.

"Come for me, Amanda. Show me how you pleasure yourself."

She felt the slow tightening within herself, the first tingling warning that an orgasm was approaching. Her eyes grew unfocused with desire, her breasts quivering as she used both hands on her pussy.

"Talk to me," she whispered, the strain of a fierce climax rapidly approaching. "Your voice . . . it excites me." She slipped a second finger into her pussy. "You make me wicked."

In a tone that was calm but authoritative, Blade said, "Come for me, Amanda. Don't deny yourself. Come . . . now."

On cue, as though the word *now* had magical qualities, she climaxed, her hands moving feverishly. Her mouth opened, but no sound came out as powerful spasms shook her curvaceous body. She was looking into Blade's eyes as she climaxed. She'd never thought looking into a man's eyes could be quite that erotic.

When the last of the convulsions shuddered through her, her hands fell from her pussy, her naked body now in an unladylike, languorous sprawl atop buffalo hides. Though she closed her eyes, she could still feel Blade's heated gaze visually caressing her.

"How do you get me to do whatever you want?" she asked softly as her breathing slowly returned to normal. "I have no doubt that if you told me to jump off a cliff, I'd do just that."

She shivered a little as he moved so that he stood between her ankles. Very slowly, he got down onto his knees, then, leaning forward, placed his hands on the buffalo hides near her shoulders.

"Guide me," he commanded.

Amanda's hands were trembling as she reached for his fiercely rigid cock and as directed, brought the knob to her still-tingling, moist entrance.

Looking up into his eyes, she whispered, "I'm yours. Do with me what you will."

She uttered a short, sharp cry of ecstasy when the unyielding cock forced her tender body to expand. Amanda pulled at Blade, wanting to feel the full weight of his powerful body pressing down against her, compressing the mounds of her breasts as his lean hips pumped with smooth precision.

When he slanted his mouth over hers, and with his cock buried full-length inside the heated confines of her pussy, she knew her next orgasm would be upon her soon, and powerful enough to shatter the illusions of a schoolteacher's sense of propriety.

A soft gasp of surprise drew Amanda from her private, erotic world and back to reality. With Blade still between her thighs and pumping hard into her, she saw that Moon had stepped into the tepee.

"Blade, stop," Amanda gasped, pushing at his shoulders.

She was utterly mortified at having been caught making love, and nearly speechless with fury at Moon's uninvited entrance into the tepee.

Blade ceased the movement of his hips and turned his upper body to look at Moon. To Amanda's growing horror, he didn't seem particularly surprised that the young widow had simply walked into his tent.

"I'm busy, Moon," he said, then turned his attention back Amanda.

"Aren't you going to do something? Tell her she's got to leave?" Amanda tried to push Blade off of her, but he was far too heavy for her to accomplish anything of significance. "Blade, aren't you going to do anything?"

His eyes were glowing with amusement when he looked down at her. "Yes, I'm going to make love to you."

"But *we're not alone.*" She spoke the final words slowly, as though he was somehow oblivious to the obvious.

Blade kissed her lightly on the tip of her nose. "She is my older brother's widow. As such, it is my responsibility to see that she has a tepee to live in, food to eat, and hides to make clothes. She lives here, Amanda."

What had been fury dissolved into abject embarrassment for Amanda. She watched as Moon, her face pale, and her expression one of unutterable sadness, walked to the opposite side of the tepee, removed her dress, then crawled naked between the buffalo hides.

Blade began moving again, withdrawing his cock to the tip before plunging back into Amanda's welcoming embrace, his torso making a light slapping sound when he'd reached full insertion. She pushed at his chest — to no avail. When she looked past the glowing embers of the small fire, she saw that Moon had kicked the blankets aside and was lying on her back with her knees up, one hand between her slender thighs while the other caressed her breasts. Amanda's gaze met Moon's and held, neither woman saying a word, yet both communicating much.

Blade's tongue made a slow circumference of her ear which brought Amanda's attention back to where it was most needed. When she turned her face toward his, he kissed her softly, tenderly, nibbling at her lower lip with his teeth as his torso pumped slowly and steadily.

It seemed impossible to Amanda that she should be making love while a woman she had just met was watching her —

and masturbating while she did so. Such a reality was unfathomable . . . but as she danced her tongue against Blade's, and felt the long, slick slide of his cock against the lips of her cunt, she had to admit that having Moon in the tepee, watching as her as she made love to Blade, heightened Amanda's excitement.

It was not the reaction that Amanda had expected of herself.

When Blade lifted his upper body, then quickly threw her legs up onto his shoulders, the orgasm she had been anticipating arrived with teeth-rattling energy and astonishing swiftness.

"Oh, yessss," Amanda purred as her body twitched through the orgasmic contractions that were intensely powerful.

Doubled nearly in half, she felt every steelish inch of Blade's cock as it sliced deep into her. As the dizziness of her orgasm passed, Amanda blinked her eyes and found herself looking up at her lover's face, dark and handsome and showing the strain of his sexual labors. And, jarringly, she saw her own bare feet on each side of his head, her feet twitching a little as she rocked under the impact of his increasingly jarring thrusts.

She turned her head to the side and saw that Moon was still staring straight at her, a hand pumping quickly between girlishly slender thighs. To watch Moon pleasuring herself and to feel Blade's incredible cock filling her at the same time was a voyeuristic and exhibitionistic thrill Amanda could not logically comprehend. Yet another orgasm approached when she heard the change in Blade's breathing. He would not last much longer.

For a split-second in time, Amanda thought of reminding her lover that he mustn't climax inside her. But then, for a reason she could not rationally define, she kept the words to herself. The fear of pregnancy being rendered mute by an emotion that lurked undefined in the shadows of her consciousness.

A moment later, he withdrew. With her legs still up on his shoulders, he unleashed a torrent of semen against her stomach and breasts. She stroked him gently and watched as a last drop of cum formed at the tip.

"You are amazing," she said in a whisper as she rubbed the final drop away with her thumb.

"No, darling, you're the one who's amazing." He leaned back so that he was sitting on his feet and eased her legs off his shoulders. "I've made another mess of you."

Amanda's reply was cut short when, on the other side of the tepee, Moon uttered a high-pitched, squealing sound, lifted her hips off the blanket, and fingered herself into what was obviously a very powerful orgasm. When her orgasm ended and her slender body was naked and relaxed on the blankets, she smiled weakly at Amanda, then rolled onto her side with her back to Amanda and promptly fell asleep.

"Does she really live here with you?" Amanda asked.

Blade picked up a small, folded towel, opened it with a snap of his wrist, then began slowly and lovingly wiping away the residue of his desire from Amanda's cooling body.

"It is tradition," he said, as though those three words explained everything. "There's not much I can do about tradition other than honor it."

Amanda closed her eyes, feeling the delicate touch of his loving hands as he cleaned her body carefully and tenderly. She loved Blade. There could be no doubting it. But equally true was that the man she loved lived in a tepee with a very attractive young squaw who was clearly ready, willing, and able to share her passion with him.

Amanda knew in her heart she would have to confront those unsettling facts soon . . . just not tonight.

CHAPTER SIX

Amanda came gently awake the next morning alone on a bed of buffalo hides. Blinking away sleep, she faintly recalled Blade kissing her eyelids and murmuring that he had work to do and that she should continue resting.

With a sleepy smile, she yawned and stretched, warmly recalling the hours of lovemaking she had gloried in the previous evening. His sexual stamina, his orgasmic discipline, and his ability to recuperate were all astonishing. Amanda couldn't remember how many times she had climaxed.

She decided that any woman who couldn't remember how many times she'd climaxed the previous evening was a very lucky woman, indeed.

Blade was an expert with his hands, with his lips and tongue, and with his cock, and he had spent hours proving his skill. He knew just how to heighten the sensual tension until it was nearly unbearable then provide the release with an orgasm that left her shaken to the core and satisfied to the marrow.

And he knew enough not to climax inside her. However much Amanda was enjoying this idyllic time with Blade and his Northern Comanche tribe, she was an unmarried woman, and he was showing no signs of relinquishing his bachelorhood.

And, of course, there was Moon, his deceased brother's widowed wife. And throughout the lovemaking, Moon had watched everything that Amanda had done with Blade . . . and though Amanda didn't want to admit it to herself, being watched by Moon had added to her excitement. Moon's presence had added a new and mysterious element to Amanda's passion, though she couldn't really define what that element was.

She didn't know what the customs were among the Northern Comanche regarding out-of-wedlock births, but in her world, such a stain on her character would prevent her from ever again teaching in a school for white children. And having an out-of-wedlock child with Indian blood would add further complications that Amanda didn't even want to consider. With this awareness always in the forefront of her consciousness, Amanda was endlessly grateful for Blade's orgasmic discipline. It was just one more thing that made her adore him.

Somewhat grudgingly, she opened her eyes to the new day. Through the smoke hole in the tepee, she could see the sun was up and had been for at least an hour. When she looked across the tepee, Moon was sitting with her legs folded beneath her. She was combing her long, silky hair with a factory-made hairbrush. She was also completely naked and clearly comfortable with her nudity.

Rather hesitantly, Amanda said, "Good morning."

Continuing to brush her hair, Moon replied, "Good morning." And, after several weighty seconds, she added a bit cattily, "Did you sleep well . . . once you decided to sleep?"

A pink blush crept into Amanda's neck and cheeks. She pushed herself into a sitting position on the buffalo robes but kept the light wool blanket wrapped around her naked body. She wasn't nearly as comfortable with her nudity as Moon appeared to be.

After deliberating for a moment on what her answer should be, Amanda finally decided on going with the truth. "Yes, I did sleep well," she said with a tone that subtly hinted at an inner sense of triumph.

Silence hung in the tepee like a black, ominous cloud. Amanda watched Moon's small, firm breasts move tautly as she brushed her hair. Would Blade prefer it if she had small breasts, like Moon's? Would he prefer her nipples to be a deep chocolate brown, instead of a pale pink? These were not comfortable questions, but ones her insecurities insisted be addressed.

"His brother knew how to make love, too."

The statement, delivered in a no-nonsense tone by Moon, made Amanda's heart seize up in her chest. After several seconds, she had to consciously force herself to exhale and inhale again. She hadn't wanted to get into a battle with Moon, but now it seemed inevitable.

"My husband was magnificent. Like Blade, he could make love all night long." Vestiges of sorrow showed in Moon's dark eyes. "He made me feel like I was the only woman in the world. His love made me feel like a . . ." She made a motion with her hands and her brow furrowed. "I don't know the right word in English. Umm . . ."

Amanda looked within herself for an answer, thinking about how Blade's lovemaking made her feel. "Like a goddess?"

Moon's face broke into a beaming smile. "Yes, like a goddess." She parted her hair down the middle and began braiding one side, but as her hands worked her hair, her eyes never left Amanda's.

"What do you want to ask me?" Amanda finally said. "I can tell there's a lot on your mind."

"Blade is a good lover, no?"

"Blade is a good lover, yes."

"He is a wonderful hunter, too. He can kill many buffalo in the summer. And in the winter, when we go into the mountains, he always finds deer and elk for us to eat. He can provide enough meat for four or five families." She sighed softly, used a piece of blue ribbon to secure the bottom of her braid, then began braiding the opposite side. "That is why I do not understand you."

Amanda's brow furrowed. "I'm not sure I know what you mean." She also wasn't sure she *wanted* to know what Moon meant, but the young widow seemed quite determined to get answers, even if Amanda didn't want to provide them.

"I do not understand why you are so selfish."

The statement made Amanda sit up a little straighter. She secured the blanket around herself, wondering if perhaps Moon's somewhat limited grasp of English might be to blame.

Amanda cleared her throat, looked away for several seconds, then replied, "In what way am I selfish?"

"To keep Blade all to yourself. He is man enough for both of us. He is a true warrior. My husband is gone, so Blade provides for my needs. But my bed is empty and my time of mourning for my husband is over. I do not see why you keep Blade all to yourself and do not share him." This time it was Moon who briefly looked away in discomfort. "Have I done something to make you dislike me?"

Moon tied off the second braid with a red ribbon and tossed both braids over her shoulders. She got to her feet, and Amanda saw that the young widow's *mons pubis* was completely smooth and hairless. Insecurities again welled up inside Amanda as she wondered whether Blade found her pubic hair—as Constance had earlier explained—a sign of poor personal hygiene. She suddenly felt a bit unclean.

"No, you haven't done anything wrong." Amanda's voice was a whisper. "Not at all."

"I have done you no wrong, yet you make love to Blade in front of me and will not let me share in your bounty. This I do not understand." She shrugged her slender shoulders, sending her breasts bobbling tautly. "There is much I do not understand about you."

The idea of being the subject of malicious gossip in the camp was appalling and appeared inevitable.

"Will you tell anyone that you saw Blade and I make love?"

Moon went rigid for a moment, looking down at Amanda with a mixture of suspicion and hurt in her chocolaty eyes. "You do not know our ways." It was a simple statement, and one that made her smile a little to herself with understanding. "Yes, that is it. You do not know our ways, and that is why you would ask such a question."

"What ways are you talking about?"

"Among the Northern Comanche, it is considered a blasphemy to speak to others what has been said or done in a tepee. It is a sin that is not easily forgiven." She pulled an unadorned buckskin dress over her head and shimmied it down over her trim hips. "That is why, whenever there are important things that must be discussed, the talk always happens with either the sun or the moon above. If they happened inside a tepee, we could not talk of them through the tribe." Moon smiled. "Come now, I will take you to the stream, and we will have our morning wash."

There were several other young women of the tribe at the stream when Amanda and Moon got there. Amanda was a little surprised at how casual the women were with their nudity, and she had to remind herself that the ways of her culture were not necessarily better than the ways of the Northern Comanche — they were simply different.

She watched as Moon twirled her hair into a rope and tied it into a knot at the base of her neck to keep it out of the water. Amanda did the same with her own hair. She followed Moon into the water, feeling only a little uncomfortable at being naked outside and in front of others.

As she bathed, Amanda was distinctly aware that other young women were looking at her. They were trying to be subtle about it, but they were indeed looking at her — and not in a friendly way.

"The others who are here," Amanda said softly, standing in the stream, very close to Moon, "they don't like me. I can see it in their eyes."

"Broken Blade is a warrior who is most prized."

Moon made the statement as though it was self-evident, though to Amanda, it wasn't. She knew he was beautiful, but it seemed that Moon was saying much more, and this made Amanda's level of insecurity escalate

"I don't understand," Amanda replied after long seconds of introspection.

"You often don't," Moon replied without hesitation, and without rancor or censure.

"We have so many differences."

"Our tepee is what we have in common," Moon said, looking Amanda directly in the eyes. "But not Broken Blade. He is yours alone." She frowned and sighed softly. "And that is something else about you that I do not understand." She sighed again. "Don't you have a special friend? A squaw who can make you feel better?"

"Special friend?"

"To help you feel better."

Amanda's eyes narrowed. Though she accepted that she and Moon were talking the same language, she was not at all certain the two of them were talking about the same thing.

She thought of asking for clarification, then decided she wasn't at all certain she wanted a more definitive answer.

Amanda had learned that sometimes in life, it was best just to not know certain things.

They bathed in the stream, using the cleansing lotion that Moon had brought with her in a small wooden bowl. The lotion was smooth and lightly scented, and Amanda discovered that after she used it, she not only felt cleaner, her skin felt smoother.

Almost on a minute-by-minute basis, Amanda was discovering that there were any things about the Northern Comanche that she wished she'd known years earlier.

She wondered how much more there was for her to learn, and even more importantly, how much time she would have to learn it.

She was distinctly aware of the fact that the clock was ticking. In many ways and regarding many things.

When Moon walked out of the water onto the shore, Amanda looked at her as though seeing her for the first time—this time without jealousy or suspicion or any of the other nebulous emotions that inevitably happen when two women and one man are involved.

She really is beautiful, Amanda thought, watching the firm, lovely movement of her pert breasts as she walked. The gentle curve of her hips, Amanda decided, was nothing less than perfection.

Amanda thought of her own voluptuous figure and wondered if Blade would find her more attractive if she were petite, like Moon, rather than the Rubenesque woman that she was. She didn't want to think too long of things like that. The more she pondered, the worse the scenarios in her mind became.

They walked back to the tepee. Blade was still gone, as they knew he would be, so they had the tepee to themselves.

Moon cast off her dress and sat cross-legged on buffalo hides, which were piled several inches thick. She began brushing her hair with a brush larger than a big man's hand that had clearly been purchased from white traders.

"So, you don't have a special friend?" Moon asked.

Amanda saw the concern in the girl's eyes. Amanda shook her head.

"I don't understand you, yellow eyes," Moon said quietly,

and a bit sadly. "You are so pretty, but you don't have a special friend to help you when you need to feel better."

Amanda's eyes narrowed. Now she was certain that she and Moon were speaking the same language, but the meanings of their words were not at all in accord.

And there's much about you that I don't understand, Amanda thought, but had the good sense to not say aloud.

Moon stopped brushing her hair. She smiled broadly and said, "Let me do your hair. And put on lotion. Maybe then you'll want me to be your special friend." She looked directly into Amanda's eyes. "I'd like to be your special friend." She smiled. "But first, take your dress off."

Amanda felt her heart skip a beat, and she reminded herself that the request itself wasn't really unreasonable.

"Lay back now and close your eyes," Moon said. "I will teach you what was taught to me." She smiled a bit sheepishly and a slight blush crept up her cheeks. "Taught to me not many seasons ago but taught to me very well. I learned much, and I remember all that I learned."

Amanda felt her heart skip a beat. A tidal wave of insecurities washed over her. When she looked into Moon's dark brown eyes, all she saw was serenity and confidence.

She knows so much more about life than me, Amanda thought. *Why didn't someone teach me the things they taught her?*

"Close your eyes," Moon said, putting her hands on Amanda's shoulders and pushing her so that she reclined on the thick bed of buffalo hides. "Let me make you feel better."

The words were like a soothing, hearty wine to Amanda. They were like a tonic that she instantly realized was necessary for her sanity. She adjusted herself on the buffalo hides, moving slightly until she was entirely comfortable. Only then, after meeting Moon's gaze one last time, did she close her eyes.

"You must let your mind go to where the moon and the stars come together," Moon said. "Think of nothing . . .

nothing but what you feel. Nothing but what I make you feel. Trust yourself to me. I know how to make you feel better."

Though her heart was pounding in her chest, and her hands were clenched into tight fists, Amanda tried to relax. There was nothing in her background that could prepare her for a moment like this. There was nothing in her life that she could look back upon that could give her some kind of understanding of how she should feel, how she should act — or was it react?

"Trust me," Moon said, her voice as soft as velvet against bare skin. "I will be your special friend, and I will make you feel better."

"Oh . . . oh, god," Amanda replied, unable to think of anything else to say.

She heard Moon whisper something in her native language, which Amanda did not speak. She wondered what the girl had said but didn't think long on it because there were more pressing things — and feelings — for her to dwell upon.

Like the soft, feminine lips that were kissing her left shoulder, and moving slowly toward her neck.

Now *that* was something to think about.

Think about very seriously, and with great concentration.

Moon moved slightly, positioning herself above Amanda, straddling her body on her hands and knees without actually touching her. The only contact of Moon to Amanda was the girl's soft, moist lips against the infinitely sensitive skin just beneath Amanda's left ear.

"Ohhh," Amanda heard herself moan. She tried to moisten her lips but discovered that her tongue was too dry to accomplish its goal. She could feel her nipples tightening and elongating, and her clitoris throbbing with escalating desire.

With the slightest move of her shoulders, Moon brushed the tips of her breasts against Amanda's. The contact was velvet-to-velvet. The breath hitched in Amanda's throat. She felt her pussy clench. Fresh nectar moistened her delicate tissue.

"Ohhh," Amanda moaned again, and she very much liked hearing the sound of passion in her own voice. She hadn't heard herself making passionate sounds very often. She suspected that with Blade and Moon now in her life, that fact was about to change.

Now it seemed as though she couldn't help herself but sigh with a wantonness that she suspected should have embarrassed her—but didn't.

She felt Moon's tongue tracing the circumference of her ear, then delicately probe inside. The sensation tickled Amanda. She smiled but managed to keep herself from giggling. It took only a couple seconds, though, for the tickling to become deeply sensual and for her body to react with desire instead of girlish, impish delight.

Moon moved her shoulders once again, and just as before—though more firmly this time—Amanda felt two small, lovely breasts brushing sideways against her own ample bosom. With a conscious effort, Amanda unclenched her fists and tried to relax enough so that she could feel everything, but relaxing was an impossibility when Moon's breasts were caressing her own, and there was a wild buzzing in her brain that simply wouldn't be quiet.

Moon kissed Amanda's cheek. She kissed several times, and Amanda sensed that the girl wanted her to turn her face so that the kiss could become more passionate.

Do it, damn it, Amanda thought, knowing that what she really wanted to do was give herself over completely and totally to Moon . . . but she couldn't. Long held inhibitions just wouldn't let her. Amanda cursed herself in a hundred different ways, furious with herself for letting her inner doubts, fears, and hidden demons prevent her from experiencing all that Moon was obviously quite willing to teach her.

But private demons could and would be cruel. They could

sabotage the most erotic moments in a woman's life and do it in a heartbeat.

Amanda felt Moon kiss the corner of her mouth. It was a soft kiss, very feminine and gentle. Then the tip of Moon's tongue lightly caressed her mouth, the girl's tongue touching both the top and bottom lip at the same time. A soft, passionate moan came from Amanda's throat, from the depths of her soul, but she did not open her mouth.

I'm sorry, thought Amanda, though she could not put the thought into words. *Moon, I'm so, so sorry.*

With an understanding of life that went vastly beyond her tender years, Moon ended her attempt to claim Amanda's mouth. She kissed her way back to Amanda's ear, tickling her inner ear some more with the tip of her tongue to ease the tension that had developed between them. Then she began making her way slowly and leisurely down Amanda's trembling body.

Moon kissed Amanda's collarbone but didn't dally long. Seconds later she was kissing the upper slope of Amanda's right breast, and as she did, Amanda could suddenly hear her own ragged, uneven breathing. She felt as though she was losing control of her body.

Her skin seemed like it was going to burst into flames at any minute. Any second now she would be nothing other than an inferno of feminine flesh utterly consumed by never-before-experienced desires that were powerful beyond comprehension.

Moon whispered something in her native language. Amanda didn't know what the words meant, and the truth of it was, she didn't really care. What was important was that she could hear the emotion in the words, the tender passion that had prompted the words—and that was all that was really important.

Then Moon's lips were inching closer and closer to

Amanda's nipple, and the girl was using her tongue to lick and caress more than she had earlier. The throbbing sensation in Amanda's nipples were so powerful it was almost painful.

She's so young, thought Amanda. *How does she know these things? Who taught her to be so . . . exquisite?*

When Moon opened her lips and captured Amanda's nipple between them, Amanda's mouth opened wide, but she did not make a sound, nor did she breathe. She opened her eyes wide and found herself looking out of the smoke hole at the top of the tepee, and at the few stars that twinkled in the night sky.

She said she was going to take me to where the moon and stars meet.

It was a pleasing thought for Amanda to have. She closed her eyes and opened her mind to all the possibilities that lay ahead.

Moon sucked gently on Amanda, taking her nipple and much of her areola into her mouth. She used her tongue deftly, licking from side to side against the nipple to elicit luscious pleasure the likes of which Amanda had not even imagined were possible. When Moon finally released Amanda's nipple, she did it with a slurping sound that, in Amanda's distorted mind, seemed amusing.

Moon kissed her way slowly across Amanda's body, down the inner slope of one breast, then up the inner slope of the other until she reached a fiercely aroused nipple that had yet to be suckled.

Moon immediately set about making sure that the nipple was suitably moistened with saliva, and that it quickly had reached maximum elongation and sensitivity. Amanda moaned her approval of Moon's behavior.

Moon was sucking on Amanda's left breast when she lowered herself so that her lower body was positioned between Amanda's tapering thighs. Amanda felt the pressure of the girl's stomach pressing against the lips of her pussy, and even more distinctly, against her pulsating clitoris. Amanda trembled as though she was cold, though quite the opposite was true. She felt like she was burning up, that her flesh was literally about to burst into flame.

CHAPTER SEVEN

Without being consciously aware of it, Amanda moved her hands and a moment later felt the satiny strands of Moon's ebony black hair beneath her palms. Could anything ever be as smooth as Moon's hair? Amanda suspected that only Blade had hair as soft as a whisper and as black as a raven's feather.

I'm the luckiest woman in the world, Amanda thought. *I have more riches than any queen in history.*

When Moon reached Amanda's belly button, she tongued it slowly and a bit teasingly. Amanda managed to keep herself from giggling, but it was not without effort. The lustful tension that Moon had created earlier diminished some, and for that Amanda was almost grateful.

Almost, but not quite.

A woman seldom gets to soar like an eagle in the warm updraft of wickedly satisfying sensations, so having the draft taken from beneath her wings was at first quite unsettling . . . and most disappointing. Rare sensations were meant to be savored.

Whatever disappointment Amanda initially experienced evaporated when Moon began kissing her lower abdomen, and—even more erotically—exposed her incisors to lightly nip at her sensitive skin as she worked her way lower, inch by inch, moving toward Amanda's most sensitive, intimate, and secret place.

Amanda felt Moon sliding her arms under her legs, then positioning her legs in the manner she wanted. Amanda's legs were now over Moon's shoulders, and the girl's arms were wound around her thighs from the underside. Moon kissed Amanda just above the entrance to her feminine temple, and once again Amanda's mouth opened into an almost perfectly shaped "O", though not so much as a peep of sound was emitted.

"Look at me."

It took several seconds before Amanda realized that she had been spoken to, and several more for her to understand that it was Moon who had spoken, and that she had asked something specific of Amanda.

"Look at me," Moon repeated, and this time she managed to push her way through Amanda's intellectual fog to actually be heard.

Amanda blinked her eyes several times to clear her vision. She looked out the smoke hole of the tepee at the stars overhead, then she looked down through the pale valley of her breasts into the chocolate brown eyes of the most beautiful girl any woman could ever wish to see between her own thighs.

"You are so precious," Amanda said in a whisper that had a certain reverential, almost religious aspect to it. "Why are you doing this for me?"

Amanda's heart nearly stopped beating when Moon turned her head and kissed the inside of her upper thigh. The girl nipped lightly with her front teeth, the sensation hinting at pain but never quite reaching that level. Then Moon soothed the flesh that she had just bitten by licking it with a warm, wet tongue that promised of pleasures that were unearthly in their extreme.

"Because I am your special friend," Moon explained quietly, with a confidence that belied her years. "And tonight, you need a special friend."

Then, as Amanda watched, Moon—with her arms around

Amanda's thighs — used her fingertips to gently separate pink lips of her pussy and brought her tongue to Amanda's clitoris.

The initial sensation was almost violent it was so powerful. The visual allure of seeing Moon's pink tongue caressing her clitoris was nearly as evocative as the sheer, magnificent physical pleasure of having her clit licked by a girl of astonishing exotic beauty.

Waves of ecstasy surged through Amanda. Her initial instinct was to close her eyes, but if she did, she would deprive herself of the voyeuristic eroticism of Moon's beautiful features which, at that moment, were on display between Amanda's spread thighs.

But not all of Moon's features were visible. Only from the nose upward. Beneath that, there was a very busy mouth that was creating havoc with every nerve ending in Amanda's body that actually mattered.

Amanda reached down and took a thick lock of Moon's hair between her index finger and thumb. She twirled the silky strands around her forefinger, stroking the strands with her thumb softly as the sexual tension inside her began to build. She could feel a climax forming in the center of her soul.

Amanda whisper, "Special friend . . ."

The two words sounded almost magical in her ears. Very much like a prayer, or words of gratitude for something divine.

She wanted to say more, but the words just wouldn't form in her brain, and even if they could, her vocal cords wouldn't allow her to articulate them.

Seconds ticked by. Time to Amanda had suddenly become a very nebulous thing, something that didn't actually measure anything relevant. She kept twisting Moon's hair around and around her forefinger while rubbing the strands with the pad of her thumb.

"That feels so . . ." Amanda said.

The sentence died in her throat when she realized that there were no words in her vocabulary which could accurately convey the totality of what she was feeling at the moment.

Amanda decided that Moon must surely be a sorceress of some kind. No mere slip of a girl could ever possibly be capable of creating such sensation without otherworldly assistance.

Amanda didn't mind if Moon was being given instructions or help from some divine being that she herself could not see or hear and did not understand. What mattered was that she was the recipient of that magnificent intervention, and since she was, she decided it was probably best to not ask too many questions.

Sometimes in life, when a woman felt this level or eroticism, it was probably best to stay silent. Not knowing answers to unasked questions can be highly erotic.

"Yesss," Amanda whispered, her eyes drifting closed despite her enjoyment of voyeurism. "You're just so . . ."

Amanda heard Moon moan. In the dim, somewhat dizzy corner of her brain that could still function, she suspected the sound the girl had just made was a sign of approval. Amanda couldn't be certain. But then, as she felt a climax approaching, she couldn't be sure of anything other than that every nerve in her body was intensely, vibrantly alive. Especially those nerve endings centered in her clitoris, which, at that moment, was between two soft lips and being caressed by a tongue of a young woman who was not only very beautiful but seemed quite determined to drive Amanda delirious with ecstasy.

"Don't," Amanda said, but then the word got choked off in her throat from the passion she felt.

Moon immediately stopped her pleasuring—which was the last thing in the world that Amanda wanted.

Amanda cleared her throat, forced herself to have the

discipline to speak the words that needed to be spoken, then in a strangely calm tone of voice said, "Don't stop."

Moon resumed her pleasuring, and seconds later, Amanda had a climax so powerful she thought her body and soul were going to turn inside-out. Waves of raw, intense pleasure shuddered through her, one after another, each one slightly less intense than the one before it.

When the last spasm had subsided, Amanda whispered, "Stop . . . I can't take any more."

"Sleep now," Moon said in a sultry purr. "You go to sleep. Everything better now."

Amanda felt herself coming awake, and she wasn't particularly happy about it. She had been resting in a state of unconscious post-orgasmic bliss. She blinked her eyes several times. Through the smoke hole in the tepee, she could see the stars overhead. She was pleased that it was still nighttime. She wasn't ready yet for morning and all the activity that went along with a new day.

She closed her eyes. There was no need to become fully awake. Not when she felt so blissfully warm and sated and . . . satisfied.

She shifted slightly on the buffalo hides that constituted her bed and became aware of a weight on her abdomen.

I'm not alone, she thought. *Moon is still with me.*

A gentle smile curled her mouth. She opened her eyes to just slits and looked through the valley of her breasts to see Moon, asleep, with her cheek against Amanda's pelvis.

Moon was holding her leg, holding it as a child might hold a cherished doll in sleep. Amanda could feel the girl's warm breath, very softly but still discernable, against her thigh.

Luscious memories of what had transpired between them came trickling slowly back into Amanda's consciousness. She felt her cheeks become warm with embarrassment. Her wanton acceptance of what Moon had been so willing to do had shocked her. She had accepted pleasures that she hadn't thought she would. She accepted those sensations greedily, metaphorically with an open mind, an open heart, and open arms.

And Moon had been everything and more than Amanda had imagined she would be.

Then Moon sighed and blinked her eyes several times. She looked up at Amanda. She gave Amanda a sleepy smile.

"You awake?" Moon asked. Her voice was muzzy with sleep.

"A little."

"Me, too. Little." Moon turned her head just enough to kiss the inside of Amanda's thigh. "Go back to sleep. Moon will help you."

Amanda tried to say something. It seemed that there were words that should be spoken, but for the life of her, she couldn't think of a single one of them. She watched, her eyes barely open, as Moon rolled onto her stomach between Amanda's thighs. She began kissing her softly, slowly, intimately.

Amanda felt her sex moistening instantly. When Moon's tongue grazed over her clitoris, Amanda sighed. She allowed her eyes to close. Her body went completely lax. It seemed as though there wasn't a bone in her body.

Amanda was half-awake and half-asleep when she had her next climax.

Once her breathing became regular and her heart had slowed to its normal rhythm, she fell asleep almost immediately.

Even in sleep there was the faintest hint of a smile curling her lips.

CHAPTER EIGHT

The posse had nine men in it. In the lead was a broad-shouldered, unsmiling man with an enormous moustache and a badge pinned to his vest. His name was Sheriff Benson, and he looked at Blade with the thinly veiled contempt of a man who sometimes must deal politely with Indians but despised having to do it. Dealing with Indians was a professional necessity that he loathed, but he had an important job and it was a necessity. It was at times like this that he hated his job.

"I came upon their trail after they attacked the train," Blade explained, standing at ease though he held his lever-action rifle cradled in his arms. "Blue Elk was responsible for the murder of one of my tribe. When I found his trail, I tracked it to where they were camped out. I slipped into camp, and that's when I killed Blue Elk."

"You killed Blue Elk, but you left the rest of the cutthroats alive." There was censure in Sheriff Benson's tone. "They just let you waltz on in and kill their leader and didn't do a damned thing about it?"

"I killed the sentry on my approach and waited for Blue Elk in his tepee. That's where I found the white woman. When Blue Elk came for her, I killed him. Then the woman and I escaped into the night." Blade looked straight into the sheriff's eyes, refusing to be intimidated by the badge on his chest. In the white man's town, that badge gave him authority. On this land, Broken Blade's word was the final judgment. "As for the rest of the men riding with Blue Elk, I do not seek revenge upon men who have done me no wrong."

"They may not have done you any wrong, but they sure as hell done wrong to all those folks on the train that they slaughtered," the sheriff replied sharply, spittle flying from his lips in his vehemence. "Why didn't you think none about them?"

Blade's expression remained passive, despite the sheriff's escalating temper. It seemed fruitless to explain that the Northern Comanche didn't feel any responsibility toward the murdered white people because the murderers had been renegade Kiowa and Cheyenne Indians. The Northern Comanche were uninvolved. He had taken his revenge upon Blue Elk and *only* upon Blue Elk because he was solely responsible for the murder of one of Blade's tribe.

The sheriff took off his dusty, sweat-stained felt hat and wiped his perspiring forehead with the sleeve of his shirt. "This white woman — she can tell us for certain who the men are that attacked the train? She can identify them?"

Blade nodded, though he wasn't at all happy about getting Amanda involved, however tangentially. He looked at the sheriff, wondering what was going through the man's mind. It was Blade's experience that whites often grouped all Indians into a single entity. This meant that the murderous behavior of one tribe might well cause all tribes to get blamed. He had heard more than a few stories about Indians being attacked on the basis of mistaken identity. That being the case, it might be safest for the Northern Comanche if he gave the posse some assistance.

"How good is your best tracker?" Blade asked.

Sheriff Benson's eyes narrowed angrily, but only for a moment. "Not too bad."

Blade lifted an eyebrow. "Not too bad, but not too good?"

Even the sheriff had to grin at that. "That's about the truth of it. He ain't too bad, but he sure as hell ain't too good, neither. Truth is, we lost their tracks miles ago."

Blade didn't bother asking the sheriff why he felt he had the right to ride through Northern Comanche territory on the foothills of the Rocky Mountains known to locals as the Blue Ice Mountains. When Indians trespassed in white territory, as often as not, it resulted in spilled blood. But whenever the white man trespassed into Indian territory, it was expected to be tolerated — a fact which irked the war chief of the Northern Comanche enormously.

"I'll be your tracker," Blade said after a moment. "Dog is no better than his brother. He just hadn't made himself my enemy, so I didn't kill him." By helping this sheriff find the killers, he could at least ensure that innocent Indians wouldn't get blamed for Dog's murderous impulses. "We'll leave at dawn."

Sheriff Benson said, "That killer's been alive too long. You help us find him, and you'll be doing a good thing." The sheriff's gaze flicked to the nearly new, well-oiled rifle in Blade's arms, and to the revolver in the holster on his left hip. "Got yourself some fine weapons."

Blade didn't bother giving an explanation for the quality of the weapons. His younger brother, whose complexion was more like Constance's than Parker's, had negotiated the deal for crates of new weapons directly with a gunsmith out of Santa Fe. He had donned a suit and necktie and used his 'white' name to conveniently circumvent any laws preventing the sale of firearms to Indians. Besides, gold had a way of making most men see only what they wanted to see.

The sheriff looked over Blade's shoulder, and an expression of confusion spread across his face. Blade turned to look in the same direction and saw Amanda approaching, her hair a spray of gold over her shoulders, the simple doeskin dress she wore pleasing him in a myriad of ways too complicated to be easily understood.

"That the gal that got kidnapped from the train?" the

sheriff asked.

Before Blade had a chance to stop Amanda, she approached the sheriff with a welcoming smile. It was obvious to Blade that she didn't share his suspicions of white men in general, and white lawmen in particular. His instinctual distrust was especially elevated when it came to posses who started out on a mission of justice with honorable intentions and regularly disintegrated into groups of men driven by revenge, bloodlust, and prejudice.

Amanda answered the sheriff's greeting. "Yes, I was kidnapped by Blue Elk's tribe." She hesitated only a moment before adding, "Blade saved my life."

"That's not a tribe," Blade corrected, ignoring the compliment. "That's a gang. An outlaw gang. Every man who rides with Dog has been banished from his tribe."

Sheriff Benson kept his attention focused on Amanda. "And you think you could identify them? You can look 'em in the face and know if they was the ones what killed all those people from the train?"

Amanda took a moment before replying, and when she spoke, it was evident she was choosing her words carefully. "Sheriff, there are very few things in this world that I'm absolutely sure of . . . but this is one of them. I'm absolutely certain that for the rest of my life I will remember the faces of the men who kidnapped me."

"Would you mind riding with us, ma'am? Once we find 'em, if you tell us you're certain they are the Injins that kilt those people on the train, that'll make it a whole lot easier for us to do what it is we got to do."

Amanda's eyes hardened. "Ride with you? Oh, sheriff, you couldn't keep me away if you tried."

The sheriff's mouth pulled up on one side. "I suppose you'll be wanting us to take you back to town when we finish with this business." It was a statement, not a question. "That's no problem for us, miss." His eyes narrowed a bit as he looked at her. "You will be coming with us, won't you, miss?"

Amanda glanced at Blade. Her returning to the white man's world had been an unasked question that hovered around them for days now.

"Maybe," she said at last. "I'm not sure what the future has in store for me."

Twenty minutes later, at the outskirts of camp though still within shouting distance, Blade clenched his teeth together so tightly his jaws ached.

"I'm going, and that's the end of the discussion." Amanda folded her arms together beneath her breasts, a glint in her eyes suggesting she would get into a fistfight with Blade before she willingly backed down to his demands.

"It's too dangerous, so you're staying here in camp, where it's safe." He took a half-step closer to her, his dark eyes darting toward the camp. If anyone saw her openly defying him, he would lose prestige among the warriors, and his leadership and manhood would be brought into question. "Now the discussion is over, so let's drop it."

"Fine. The discussion is over." But as his expression softened, she added, "I'm going with the posse. We don't need to discuss it anymore."

"Goddamn it, Amanda," Blade hissed under his breath, using the curse that the priests always took so much umbrage with. "Why won't you listen to reason?"

It was her apparent calmness that infuriated him the most. She was just standing there, quietly, and consistently refusing to follow his orders. He was the son of a chief, and a chief in his own right, and women simply didn't disobey him. Didn't she realize that?

"Blade, I think you should calm down some," Amanda said conversationally. "You really look agitated, and it's frankly undignified."

Closing his eyes, Blade inhaled deeply and let his breath out slowly. "You are the most stubborn woman the world has ever known."

"Perhaps I don't always do what you want," Amanda replied sweetly. "But when it comes to making love, you've got to admit I do whatever you ask. Gladly, too."

Despite himself, Blade had to smile. "Promise me you won't tell anyone that I let you openly defy me and that you won an argument. My reputation would be in shambles."

Blade saddled Tikki and rode out of camp, furious with the hot-blooded, passionate, mind-bendingly stubborn yellow eyes woman who had entered his life without being invited and seemed determined to do whatever she wanted to, with or without Blade's approval. As a man long accustomed to having his instructions followed instantly, Amanda's stubborn determination to make her own choices was more than mildly vexing.

He rode alone, eastward toward the lush, verdant mountains, and when he was miles from camp, he dismounted and let Tikki drink from a cool stream and eat the rich grass. To the east were the Blue Ice Mountains, much of which his tribe — under his mother's maiden name — already owned. Eventually, from the gold that Blade and a select group of warriors were extracting from the mountain, he hoped to own enough land and have enough gold in the bank to ensure the security of the Northern Comanche for the turbulent coming years.

The safety and security of his tribe meant everything to Blade. That emotion had been foremost in his great-grandfather's heart when he took a small band of followers and separated from the Comanches of Texas, moving northward with a Jesuit priest into more moderate climates. The safety and security of the Northern Comanche was the driving force behind the frequent trading done between the tribe and the white man. Quite literally for decades, in an effort to ensure the safety and survival of the Northern Comanche, the tribe was forced to deal directly with its most pressing and persistent enemy — the white man.

These thoughts plagued Blade's tranquility as he sat on verdant land that he and his tribe owned.

But there was something else that haunted his peace of mind. That *something else* was pale-skinned and curvaceous, and her golden blonde hair reflected the sunlight with the luminescence of the sun itself. Her smile had the ability to go through his eyes and hit him straight in the heart. The sound of her laughter was the purest form of music that he'd ever heard. Her kisses were the very essence of passion's promise.

And Blade was in love with her.

He had just now fully realized it, and the awareness horrified him.

Damn.

Damn it all to the Hell that the Jesuit priests always warned about.

Blade hadn't counted on falling in love. He had too much to do for him to allow himself to fall in love. There were too many people who counted on him. He had too much responsibility for him to take on the additional burden of love.

He closed his eyes and sought the advice of the spirits. Perhaps they had answers, for he was a man sorely in need of them.

He had hoped for a vision to give him answers, but he didn't get one. Instead, a small voice whispered inside his mind . . . telling him that Amanda had to leave. He had to return her to the white man's world. To do otherwise was to jeopardize the tribe. He had responsibilities that were bigger than himself, more important than his own wants and wishes. He had to remember his responsibility for nearly a thousand men, women, and children.

So, Amanda had to go back to her world once Dog and his band were dealt with. When the posse headed home, she would go with them, back to the life she knew. She would go back to her world, and he had to stay in his.

It was as simple as that.

Blade made a point of not returning to camp until after sundown. As he approached his tepee, he could hear feminine laughter from inside. He smiled. Apparently, the animosity between Amanda and Moon had been short-lived, a fact for which he was grateful. He didn't need any more confrontations in his life.

On the next morning, with any luck at all, Amanda would oversleep and he'd be able to convince Sheriff Benson she was ill and that they'd have to go after Dog and his band of cutthroats without her. Once Dog was dealt with, Blade could return her to her white world so that he could concentrate on his personal duties to the Northern Comanche.

He stepped through the entrance and found Moon and Amanda sitting with their legs folded beneath them, facing each other as they played the hand-game of rochambeau. When Blade had played the game during his university days—the loser invariably having to buy the next round of drinks—he discovered in the white man's world it was called Paper-Rock-Scissors. But it was exactly the same game. Entirely different cultures: exactly the same game—independently created.

Both women looked up at him, a beaming smile coming from each.

"I see that you two have gotten over your differences," Blade said a bit cautiously.

"I've had a great time with Moon. We discovered we have much in common," Amanda said.

For a moment, Blade took in the feminine beauty on display before him. Neither Moon nor Amanda was making any effort at trying to be sexy, and perhaps that was the reason why their physical beauty struck him so powerfully.

Seated with their legs folded caused their doeskin dresses to split at the hip, giving him a view of beautiful and feminine legs, one set being dark and slender, the other pale and shapelier. And though Moon's bosom was such that she did not have much skin on display, Amanda's neckline, though not low-cut by any means, still showed a mouthwatering amount of creamy pale breasts he found impossible to resist. Amanda's hair had been brushed, parted down the center, and put into two braids — the same hair style all the squaws of the Northern Comanche wore.

"Have you eaten?" Amanda asked. "We were expecting you hours ago."

"No, I haven't."

Blade hadn't planned on being gone as long, either. He had completely missed the evening meal. He had needed the additional time to come to terms with his personal responsibilities to the tribe and the unpleasant actions he had to take to fulfill those responsibilities.

"Moon and I saved a bowl for you. It's not hot anymore, but it's still warm. It's really quite savory." Amanda lifted a buffalo hide and revealed a pottery bowl with a lid. "Sit down over there and we'll help you."

Blade's brow furrowed. Amanda wasn't really a difficult woman to be with, but there had to be some reason for her to be *this* accommodating. And there was an amused gleam in Moon's eyes that Blade couldn't account for, a devilish twinkle he hadn't seen since before her husband's death when she was an ecstatically married newly-wed.

He sat cross-legged on the buffalo hides that constituted his bed. Amanda and Moon quickly sat down with him, one at each knee.

"It's awfully good," Amanda said, handing Blade the bowl. "I had a bowl myself. I'm learning to like your food."

Blade took a wooden spoon from Moon and tried the stew. It was, as promised, delicious. He knew it would be. What he didn't know was what the women had planned during his absence. The mischievous twinkle in their eyes told him they were up to something. Probably something naughty. Naughtiness practically oozed out of the women's pores.

"You should get comfortable." Amanda tugged free the leather thong that held on one of Blade's moccasins.

"Yes, you should be comfortable," Moon added as she removed his other moccasin. This left him wearing only his buckskin breechclout.

"You like the stew?" Amanda asked solicitously. "Eat. It'll make you strong and give you stamina."

Looking straight into her emerald-green eyes, he asked, "What's going on in that clever and devious mind of yours?"

She took the bowl and spoon from him. "Let me feed you," she said, her voice now a sultry purr. She dipped the spoon into the stew and brought it to his mouth. "Open up."

"I can feed myself," Blade replied, but that didn't stop him from opening his mouth. She spoon-fed him, and as he chewed the sumptuous buffalo meat in the gravy-like stew juices, he became aware of Moon's small hands upon his left thigh. But then Amanda had another spoonful at his mouth. "Wait, I—"

She silenced him with a mouthful of stew as small fingertips, touching as delicately as a butterfly's feet, walked up his naked thigh. Before those slender brown fingers reached the top of his leg, there was a distinct tightening in his breechclout, and he had curiously cleared his throat somewhat nervously three times in the previous thirty seconds.

"Do I want to know what you women have been talking about in my absence?" Blade asked, his cheek puffed out because Amanda continued to ladle the stew into his mouth and seemed hell-bent on seeing to it that he ate every last morsel in the bowl.

"I've been talking with Moon, and she explained some of the . . . um . . . customs of the Northern Comanche that are . . . well, let's just say that they're different from what I'm familiar with." When she looked at Moon, there was an affectionate warmth in her eyes that hadn't been there before. She reached out and casually eased Moon's braided hair over her shoulder, and Blade felt a rush of excitement come to life in his veins at the innocent contact between the women.

"Moon's had a very difficult time of it since the death of her husband." Amanda placed her left hand lightly on Moon's smooth, naked thigh. The sight of it caused Blade's erection to spring to life swiftly, vibrantly. She leaned forward and kissed him briefly and lightly on the lips, then sat back. "Moon, perhaps you could help Blade get more comfortable. He seems . . . um . . . to have outgrown his clothing."

With a tug on the braided cord holding his breechclout secure, Moon released the knot and pulled the entire front of the buckskin garment away. His cock, not yet fully erect yet still impressive in size, bobbed when freed, coming to rest warm and heavy against his thigh.

"Blade, pay attention," Amanda said a bit scoldingly, holding yet another spoonful of stew close to his mouth. "You've only got a little bit left in the bowl, and you need to eat so that you have plenty of strength."

"I can believe that," Blade replied with a sardonic grin, turning his face toward Amanda.

He was taking the stew from the spoon when Moon's lips — soft, wet, and warm — surrounded the head of his cock.

In that instant, he responded to her oral caress with impressive new dimensions. He looked at Amanda and saw her watching Moon as she pleasured him. Jealousy and pain flared in her eyes, flaming like a sulfur matchhead.

Instantly, he worried that he was about to have one hellacious fight on his hands, but then Amanda closed her eyes and gave her head and shoulders a little shake as though to physically release disturbing emotions. When she opened her eyes again and looked into his, the emerald-green fire that so enraptured the warrior from the very beginning of their time together was blazing magnificently once again.

Now, in her eyes, there wasn't so much as a hint of anger.

Blade started to look down at Moon, but Amanda put her hand under his chin and raised his face. "So, what did you do when you rode out of camp today?" Her tone was the essence of innocence.

The sensation of butter-soft lips traveling back and forth over the crown and some of the shaft of his erection was creating a spike of lust that demanded all his concentration, but Amanda seemed unwilling to allow him that luxury. With some difficulty, he swallowed the last of the stew.

"Well?" she prodded, setting the bowl and spoon aside. "You must have done something. You were gone for hours."

Blade set his hand lightly atop Moon's slowly nodding head, neither hindering nor guiding her movements. The texture of her ebony hair against his palm was softer than silk. The gentle moans that emanated from the girl was a carnal symphony that added significantly to the dimensions of his erection.

"Kiss me," Amanda said, placing both hands on his cheeks to position him properly and hold him steady.

It was a hungry, demanding kiss, a bold and declarative statement of her burgeoning passion. In a flash, Blade remembered how with her first kisses she had been timid and uncertain. Now she was a woman in charge, passionately de-termined to give and receive all the pleasure the human body was capable of.

Thirty seconds later, Amanda pushed Blade away, grabbed her doeskin dress, tugged the soft leather over her head, then cast the garment disdainfully across the tepee.

"Kiss me," she demanded again. Only this time she lifted her left breast as she hooked her hand behind Blade's neck and guided him to her pink nipple. When his lips surrounded the crest of her breast and his tongue scraped the erect nipple, she rolled her head back on her shoulders and purred. "Yesss!"

CHAPTER NINE

Amanda held Blade tightly to her breast, her eyes open but hazy with lust as she stared at the gorgeous man who was busily sucking on her nipple.

After several seconds, she turned her gaze to Moon. Her head was continuing to bob up and down as she took much of Blade's exquisite cock into her mouth and throat. Jagged-edged jealousy surged through Amanda, and for several agonizing seconds she was entirely convinced that she'd made the biggest mistake of her life in thinking she could share Blade with another woman. The emotions she had for him, though assuredly carnal, included something more inclined toward love than mere lust — and the heart, as she was beginning to understand, wasn't very good at sharing. At least not when it came to sharing Blade.

She was fighting against these emotions, and she wasn't at all certain if she was winning.

"I want some of that."

Amanda heard herself say the words, though she hadn't consciously thought them. And unless she was completely mistaken, there was a distinct cattiness to her tone she surely wouldn't have approved of ahead of time. She clenched her teeth, fighting against emotions green and uncharitable, as she watched Moon nibble down the shaft of Blade's thick cock, the lovely young widow's eyes closed as she pleasured with practiced ease and expertise.

The fact that she loved having Blade's cock in her mouth was obvious. Simply without question.

It was a novel experience for Amanda. Though she had performed fellatio previously, she had never wanted to take an erection into her mouth. She did it, but only because it was expected or demanded of her. She did it because it was an obligation.

But now, everything about her emotions in conjunction with the warrior named Broken Blade were entirely new. He inspired an adventurous spirit, especially when it came to matters of a carnal nature. But then, everything about Blade had a carnal nature to it.

Easing her breast out of Blade's mouth, Amanda bent to flick her tongue across his nipple. She heard his sharp intake of breath and knew then that his nipples were every bit as sensitive as her own. With this in mind, Amanda kissed across the hard-muscled surface of his naked chest and sucked on his other nipple. And when she heard his low, throaty moan of approval, the lips of her pussy swelled and creamed in anticipation of being forced to stretch to accommodate his flaring cock.

Amanda was beginning to suspect that there were times with the perfect man when masculine force could be worthy of nothing less than a spine-jarring climax. She'd never known that until that very moment.

Moon seemed not to have heard her since she continued to feast upon Blade's extravagant manhood—a fact which irked Amanda to the quick. Sliding down his powerful body, she put a hand on Moon's shoulder and, with unladylike determination, simply pushed the slender widow with so much force that she tumbled backward onto her bottom.

"Sorry," Amanda said with a noticeable lack of sincerity in her tone. "It's my turn now."

She straddled Blade's left leg with her knees then positioned herself over the cock that stood up tall and proud. She blew her breath lightly upon the flaring crown. The taut knob flexed, and the skin stretched even more tightly over the swollen inner core.

An opaque pearl of fluid formed at the slit, and Amanda purred kittenishly as she licked off the salty droplet. The flavor was not one that Amanda particularly appreciated, but with nascent jealousy continuing to flow more heatedly through her veins with each passing second, she wouldn't dream of putting her negative thoughts into her expressions. She pushed her lips over the massive crown, then began nibbling down the shaft, using only her lips and tongue, careful to sheath her teeth from touching the sensitive flesh.

Amanda took Blade to the back of her mouth. She knew she couldn't take him as deeply as Moon had, and this fact infuriated her. But when she tried to take his unyielding flesh into her throat—as Moon must surely have done, at least to some extent—her body protested, and she was forced to lift her head quickly. She coughed and sputtered. It took several seconds to compose herself.

"Let me," Moon said, almost lunging for Blade's suddenly available erection.

Amanda had Blade back in her mouth in an instant, rather churlishly depriving Moon of the opportunity to prove she was better at giving the warrior pleasure with her mouth. Amanda nibbled lightly with her lips on the thick, somewhat oval-shaped shaft as she used her tongue against the underside of the crown. Blade groaned softly of his approval, and she answered him with a moan that was perhaps slightly louder than warranted.

As she descended upon him, the heavy weight of her breasts slid against his hard thigh, thick with muscle from having lived a life on horseback. She gave her shoulders a little shake, slapping her breasts against his leg, and he responded with a sigh of pleasure.

Tilting her head back with her lips still encircling his cock,

Amanda looked up into his dark eyes. She saw the strain of sexual tension in his features, and the expression gave her sudden confidence, and a certain sense of charitable generosity returned.

She released Blade with a wet slurping sound, looked up at the man who had taught her so much about so many aspects of life, and saucily declared, "What do you think of me now?"

Amanda's blunt question caused Blade's jaw to clench. She, vastly amused at her own burgeoning sexual confidence, made a lewd spectacle of licking the head of Blade's cock for several seconds before she said, "Moon has been explaining some of the differences between our cultures. She's been lonely. It seems to me that you and I might be of some assistance to her."

Amanda wasn't in the least bit annoyed when Blade rather brutishly grabbed her by the hair and hauled her up so that he could give her a fierce kiss. It was when he was at his most barbaric and his least civilized that Amanda's body reacted instinctively, joyously, and spontaneously. The warrior in him was what excited Amanda more than anything else, making her juices flow freely to the tingling lips of her pussy. Her clitoris literally ached with the want of him.

With her hair still wrapped around his fist, Blade ended the kiss. He stared intently into her eyes, and for a moment Amanda wondered if she had done something wrong. The sounds of a sensual, wet fellatio being passionately given drifted to Amanda's ears, letting her know that Moon had taken advantage of the opportunity presented to her. Together, Amanda and Blade looked down and watched as Moon sucked his cock with a passion that was as visible as it was physical.

Amanda kissed him one last time, then looked into Blade's eyes and gave the merest of approving nods. Blade removed

Moon's doeskin dress, then stretched her out onto the buffalo hides. Looking at Moon, Amanda again felt a twinge of jealousy and uncertainty. Dusky-skinned, extremely petite, Moon's body was almost the antithesis of her own. When Blade was perched over Moon, bending low to kiss her left nipple, she appeared even smaller in contrast to the powerful warrior.

Blade flicked his tongue over Moon's blunt, erect nipple, and Amanda squeezed her eyes tightly shut against the jealous pain. She turned her face away. Seconds passed. A battle raged inside her. She was hooked on the horns of a dilemma, part of her wanting to be generous to Moon, and part of her wanting to be exclusive to Blade.

Amanda opened her eyes just as Blade eased his middle finger into Moon's damp cleft, smiling when the young widow moaned with rapidly escalating passion before he withdrew the glistening finger altogether.

Raising his hand to Amanda's mouth, he said, "Taste her."

Amanda resisted. She didn't know why, but she did not submit immediately to Blade's demand. But as was so often the case, his willpower and Amanda's own sensual curiosity were her undoing. She parted her lips, and he eased his finger into her mouth. She could taste the young widow's honey as he eased the finger back and forth between her lips, pantomiming a fellatio in progress. Amanda moaned softly, letting him know she was willing to do whatever he asked.

Blade hooked his hand behind her neck and pulled her close. After a brief kiss, his lips brushed against her ear. "You don't want this to happen. I can see it in your eyes."

Amanda shook her head in negation of his statement and replied in a voice so low that only he could hear, "Moon has been without a loving man for so long . . ."

He smiled, paused a moment to watch Moon as she waited in a half-conscious sensual haze, then looked up again at

Amanda. "Do you trust me?" he asked in that wickedly tempting way of his.

For a moment, Amanda closed her eyes. It seemed to her terribly unfair that he should be so capable of making the world conform to his wishes. He was a man who seemed to *always* get what he wanted. But she knew, both instinctively and from experience, that when he guided her actions, her own sexual satisfaction was guaranteed.

Blade lay down beside Moon on his buffalo hide bed. For a moment, Amanda was afraid she couldn't continue. But he smiled reassuringly and made a gesture for her to lay down on the opposite side of Moon.

"Such beautiful maidens," Blade said, his gaze going slowly over both women.

"But I am not a maiden," Moon said quickly, softly, sincerely. "I am a widow."

"So different and so beautiful." The flattering gleam in Blade's eyes said her status within the tribe didn't matter to him.

He dipped his head, sealing his lips over Moon's mouth. His mouth opened, and Amanda felt her own heart seize up briefly.

"Your turn," Blade said when the kiss ended, sliding his hand around Amanda's neck to pull her so that she was leaning over Moon.

Whatever inhibitions Amanda may have had vanished the instant Blade's lips came in contact with her own and his moist tongue began its tantalizing dance of ultimate domination and seduction. She moaned soulfully, distinctly aware of the places her naked body touched Moon's.

By the time the kiss with Blade ended, Amanda's emotions were spinning drunkenly. His hand was still at the back of her neck, and after a quick kiss on the tip of her nose, he pushed her head down toward Moon.

"Now it's your turn to kiss Moon."

Amanda hadn't meant to gasp, but the simple declaration caught her by surprise. She looked down at Moon, seeing the young woman in a way she never had before, taking in the softness of her lips and the loveliness of her dark eyes — the girl seemed so different now that Blade was there, so very near, watching with the intensity of an eagle on the hunt. This wasn't at all like when she had been alone with Moon.

Blade's presence made everything different.

She resisted the pressure of Blade's hand, but only briefly. If this was what Blade wanted her to do, kissing Moon while he watched seemed a small chore to please the man she adored.

Very slowly, Amanda bent over Moon. She felt the heaviness of her breasts come into contact with Moon's much smaller bosom. Amanda's body responded favorably in an instant. Her nipples became even more erect. The slick nectar of her passion flowed freely to the lips of her pussy.

"You're so lovely," she whispered before slanting her mouth over the young widow's.

Amanda immediately came to the conclusion that kissing another woman while Blade was watching was significantly different than kissing a man — not necessarily better or worse, just *different*. Moon's mouth was much smaller than Blade's, her lips softer.

Having Blade there added a significant level of eroticism to the experience.

Amanda was quickly learning to delight in the differences between kissing a man she adored and a girl she delighted in. After a few light kisses, Amanda pressed her mouth more firmly against Moon's. Within a minute, she eased her tongue between Moon's lips, heightening the intimacy between them as a lifetime of inhibitions regarding taboo pleasures was no longer pushed to the edges of her consciousness, they simply vanished altogether as though they'd never existed.

A shiver went through Amanda as she played her tongue against Moon's while blindly reaching for a small, firm breast. When she lightly pinched Moon's nipple, the two women shared a mutual moan without ending the kiss. Amanda was taking unprecedented enchantment in giving pleasure to her new friend while knowing that Blade was watching everything that she was doing.

Moon flinched briefly but wrapped both arms tightly around Amanda's neck, hugging her tightly. With some effort, Amanda extricated herself from the young woman's boa constrictor embrace and discovered what had caused the girl's strong, physical response. While Amanda and Moon had been sharing a series of deeply intimate kisses, Blade had slipped down on the buffalo hides and repositioned himself between brown, slender thighs.

Amanda was momentarily shocked but wickedly aroused at seeing Blade using his lips and tongue upon Moon's delicate, hairless sex. Seeing his handsome face wedged between Moon's legs, his eyes closed in either pleasure or concentration, was perhaps the most shockingly erotic thing Amanda had ever seen. Moon's low moans of pleasure were almost continuous, and Amanda smiled because she knew from experience the kind of spine-jarring climaxes Blade was capable of producing with just such intimate kisses.

Propped on an elbow, Amanda let her gaze go leisurely over Moon's naked body, taking in the petite beauty of her bosom, the areolas small and distinct from the rest of the breasts, the nipples fiercely erect with passion, her stomach flat, the slender legs now parted to accommodate Blade as his tongue worked sensually between the lust-enflamed lips of her pussy.

Slowly, almost in a trance, Amanda bent down once again, but this time instead of feasting upon Moon's delicious mouth, she captured the girl's nipple between her lips. She sucked tenderly upon the small, feminine button of flesh, her mind in a whirl as she tried to comprehend the fact that she was tasting a woman's nipple and taking profound pleasure in the act. Her oral caress elicited an immediate gasp and sigh from Moon, informing Amanda that her actions were appreciated.

Strong fingers pushed into her golden hair, the hand large, tugging on her hair, its action commanding. Following Blade's guidance, she kissed down the front of Moon's body, pausing briefly to play her tongue into the dimpled belly button that whispered for attention.

The nearer to Blade that Amanda moved, the harder her heart hammered against her ribs. Blade's presence, his masculinity, added something new that hadn't been there when Amanda and Moon had been indulging exclusively in their feminine world of sensual splendor.

"Kiss me," Blade said when Amanda was very close, "and you'll taste Moon's passion."

Hearing the bold words caused the breath to catch in Amanda's throat. She folded her knees beneath her and met Blade's gaze, knowing hers must be filled with apprehension.

"You'll do fine," he said, once again amazing Amanda at how accurately he could read her thoughts. "Just do to her what I've done to you."

"But—"

Blade silenced her protest by kissing her on the mouth, his lips tasting of Moon's intimate honey. Amanda kissed him for a long time, becoming more excited with each passing second, as she always did whenever his passionate attention was directed at her. When the kissing ended, he repositioned her so that she was on her elbows and knees, her face close to Moon's feminine temple. Blade moved lower on the buffalo hides.

She could smell the tantalizing aroma of a young woman's

lust. It triggered in her an instant, primitive, primordial response which was so powerful that for a moment it made Amanda shiver.

For several seconds, Amanda simply looked at Moon. The girl's pubic mound was completely free of any hair, the skin smooth and velvet soft, the petals glistening wetly in the dim light of the tepee. Seconds ticked by, and just when Amanda thought she'd have to apologize for not following through with what was clearly expected of her, she felt Blade's hands on her bottom, pulling her hips downward. A moment later, when his mouth came in contact with her pussy, a shiver went through her as his probing tongue separated the lips of her sex and grazed over her clitoris.

Amanda suddenly realized that the best antidote to inhibition was extreme desire.

If Blade wanted Amanda to give Moon exotic pleasure while he was there, then she was willing to do it. To please him, to entertain him, to impress him—Amanda was willing to do anything. Anything at all. With a shiver and a sigh, as Blade's tongue moved slickly over her own clitoris, Amanda lowered her head and brought her mouth to Moon's pussy.

Amanda realized both instantly and instinctively that there was nothing so delicious on the tongue as a taboo pleasure that could never be talked about.

She was quite certain she was the luckiest woman in the world.

Moans and sighs of carnal excess filled the tepee. Amanda went about pleasuring Moon, clumsily because of her inexperience, though she went at the task of eliciting a satisfying orgasm for the young widow with dogged persistence and limitless energy. It was easy for Amanda to lose concentration, since Blade was doing to her what she was doing to Moon—and Blade most definitely had significant experience in this sort of adventuring.

Amanda was the first to reach orgasm, though Moon did not trail her by many seconds. With her arms wrapped around Moon's naked, slender thighs, she kept her mouth pressed tightly to the girl's pussy as she herself bucked and writhed in ecstasy against Blade's mouth, rippling waves of pure emotion shuddering through her system.

Only when Moon was gasping and begging for her to stop did Amanda lean back and put an end to her oral caresses.

As soon as Moon had finished with her climax, Blade turned his attention to Amanda again—to her complete delight. He grabbed her by the upper arms and twisted her around on the buffalo hides, her prone body half atop Moon even as he positioned himself between her tapering thighs.

His first invasion was nearly full-length, brutish in its intensity, his practiced charm having been stripped away by her wanton sense of sexual adventurousness and Moon's delicious enticements. He stretched himself over Amanda, his chest glistening with perspiration, his mouth slick with her honey.

"Take me," Amanda whispered, finding it arousing to feel Moon's naked thigh beneath her head like a pillow as Blade's thick cock filled her completely. Her world of sensuality was expanding rapidly, and it was thrilling for her. "Take me any way you want me."

Amanda was primed for the next orgasm, which struck with sledgehammer force on the fourth stroke of Blade's exquisite cock into her pussy. The scent of Moon's arousal significantly heightened Amanda's own readiness for culmination. She suspected she should feel guilty for some reason, but this thought didn't stay with her long when mind-boggling pleasure was inundating her senses.

She pulled Blade down so that his chest crushed her breasts. This was how she loved him the most—when his weight was on her and she could feel his great strength dominating her both literally and metaphorically. She could tell he was throwing everything he had at her, his muscular body pounding her into the buffalo hides, the thickly-veined shaft of his relentless cock tugging at the lips of her cunt and rubbing ever so close to her clitoris.

Opening her eyes, she discovered that Moon was sitting up with her hands behind her. Amanda looked into the girl's dark brown eyes as she was tossed once more into the abyss of sensual excess, her body wracked by powerful orgasmic spasms that left her weak and gasping for air. Her climax was almost violent in its intensity . . . and she couldn't have wanted for anything more.

"Wait," she whispered. "P-Please . . . I need to . . . catch my . . . breath." She stroked Blade's ebony hair, smoothing the thick strands away from his face. "You're so . . ."

Words failed Amanda. All she was absolutely certain of was that she didn't want this evening to end, that she wanted it to go on and on so that Blade could teach her all the ways it was possible to give and receive pleasure.

Whatever the question, Blade was always the answer.

Moon eased her leg out from beneath Amanda's head. Amanda let out a small moue of disappointment and was distinctly aware of the fact that she no longer had the scent of Moon's passion tickling her senses.

"Now, my darling," Amanda purred to Blade, feeling the hard length of his cock filling her, "I think it is time you concentrated on your own pleasure."

"You have no idea how much it pleases me to see you passionate. You got excited by tasting Moon, didn't you?" Blade said, his words hardly more than a whisper though their impact on Amanda's senses was a roaring thunderclap.

"You liked watching me?" Amanda asked. Her tone was ambiguous, her self-confidence in such matters fragile in the extreme.

Blade began moving his hips, the long retreat of his cock done slowly so that she could feel each individual nerve ending being tantalized. She pulled his head down, needing his chest against her tingling breasts. When she felt his teeth nipping at her throat, she let out a squeal of submissive delight.

It was especially erotic when Blade danced the tightrope that separated pleasure from pain. He had taught her that, and only he was trusted enough for her to go into that dangerous territory.

With his ear close to her lips, Amanda whispered, "Fuck me hard. If I don't have bruises, it means you didn't try hard enough to please me."

His hands gripped her ass, long fingers mauling her flesh as he lifted her hips upward to meet his ramrod downward thrusts. Ever the dutiful lover, Blade had been given a demand by Amanda and he fulfilled that command spectacularly, his lean hips pumping between her thighs as his cock plunged and retreated, the roar of his labored breathing hot and moist against the side of her face.

Amanda's next orgasm was even more powerful and draining than those previously experienced. She was just beginning that slow, blissful, post-orgasmic descent from the emotional stratosphere when Blade thrust full-length into her, plunging deeply then withdrawing completely as his guttural, strangled growl of ecstasy burst from his lungs. Amanda felt him shudder as he released his passion, leaving four rivers of sperm from her chin to her navel.

"Yes," she purred, stroking the back of his head as his body went lax atop hers. "I love the sound that you make when you come." When Blade started to roll off Amanda, she tightened her legs around him. "Not yet. I love the way it feels to have you on top of me."

She was blissfully aware that his sperm was on her. When he propped himself on his elbows to take some of his weight off her, Amanda looked up into his dark eyes, wondering what thoughts were going through his mind.

"You're mine now," he said, answering her unasked question. "You're mine."

His arousal had lost only a portion of its stature after his orgasm, and to Amanda's amazement and delight, she felt it grow to full-length once more against her belly.

"You're mine," Blade repeated, a little louder than before. "You're mine. Do you hear me? You're mine."

CHAPTER TEN

Thank goodness he didn't come in my mouth, Amanda thought as she looked down her body at the thick, creamy rivers of sperm that now ran from her chin to her navel. She hadn't thought it possible that a single man could create that much cum during an orgasm. She suspected the man she'd known in the past was lacking, though she hadn't known it until Blade became a part of her world.

Amanda was learning, and very rapidly, that the man named Broken Blade was unlike any man she, or any other woman, had ever met.

The thought made her shiver.

She looked at Moon. The girl's eyes were half closed, and the expression on her face was one of sublime satisfaction.

I've pleased her, Amanda thought, finding herself a little surprised that she was quite proud of herself for having done so.

She watched as Blade eased his body between herself and Moon. He moved slowly. There wasn't a part of his powerful, naked body that wasn't glistening with perspiration.

The urge to taste that sweat, to run her tongue over parts of his body that she found most delectable, was almost overpowering for Amanda.

She didn't lick Blade's body, but she wished at that moment that she had the courage to.

Amanda looked at the girl. Moon's eyes were deep brown and when Amanda looked into them, she couldn't read any coherent thought.

Moon's in a daze, Amanda thought. *A sexual intoxication.*

113

Amanda had heard about a sexual stupor once, when she was at a party and the wine had been flowing rather freely and inhibitions about talking about such things seemed to slip away.

She wished with all her heart and soul that she could experience such a haze herself. She wanted to know what it was like, first-hand and without having to be told by anyone else, what it was like to sexually be in a fog, in a state of semi-consciousness where nothing existed. Everything else was extraneous. Everything else was excess emotional baggage that didn't need to be carried around.

Amanda moved so that she was next to Moon. She found the girl's body to be warm and tantalizing against her own. With a finger she smoothed a lock of hair away from Moon's lovely brown eye, then ran the pad of her finger across the girl's eyebrow.

"You know you're lovely, don't you?"

Amanda saw the doubt in the girl's eyes, and it triggered in herself an instantaneous anger at the world the likes of which she'd never before experienced.

With more force in her voice this time, she asked again, "You know you're beautiful, don't you?"

Achingly long seconds ticked by before Moon stretched her arms and legs in a luxurious manner, then issued a long sigh of sexual satisfaction. She appeared to be a young woman without a single, solid bone in her body.

"Now I do," Moon said. "In my world, we have many gods, and I want you to know that I will thank every one of them for having you in my life." Moon sighed again. "I will thank all the gods that there are for you and Blade. I thought that pleasure was only something that I could think back about until you came into my life." She sighed. "You make me feel blessed. I'd never felt that way after my husband was killed. Then you two came into my life."

Amanda felt her own sexual confidence rising by the second. She looked at Moon, naked and brown and lovely by any measure that anyone could possibly make and said to herself that this night was a long way from over . . . and that she herself was galaxies away from ending her experimentation into the world of forbidden eroticism.

Amanda ran the pad of her thumb over Moon's left eyebrow, then her right. She could feel her own sexual self-confidence wavering, sometimes becoming stronger, but then a moment later become weaker.

She was in scary emotional territory. There was nothing about what was happening in the tepee that Amanda had any real experience with. Yes, she'd had her night of exquisite passion with Moon, but on that occasion, she had been the passive recipient, always on the receiving end of bliss, but never of the giving end, never the provider of erotic sensations that boggled the mind and sated the senses.

"Kiss her."

It took a moment for Amanda to realize that Blade had spoken. Actually, he had more than merely spoken—he had issued a command. He had told Amanda what she must do, what action she must take.

When Blade spoke in a manner like that, what he said was not a suggestion that could either be followed or ignored. It wasn't a question that might or might not be answered. They were commands that had to be followed.

This awareness made a shiver slither through Amanda. She was consciously aware of the fact that she had never met a man who was even remotely in the same category as the Northern Comanche warrior named Broken Blade. In her mind, he alone stood at the summit.

Amanda eased the fingers of her right hand beneath the thick, silky ebony hair at the back of Moon's head. For a moment she just caressed the girl's scalp, marveling at how soft and luxurious her hair was. She looked into the girl's eyes, and when she did, she saw a gleam of pleasure. Whatever was about to happen, Amanda realized, was with Moon's complete, total, and uninhibited consent.

"You're so beautiful," Amanda whispered, her lips close enough that she could undoubtedly feel the heat of Amanda's breath against her face.

She watched as Moon closed her eyes in silent surrender. Amanda felt her own sex clench in response. There was nothing in this forbidden menage in a tepee that Amanda did not welcome with all her heart and soul and passion. She could feel herself become more than what she had been. She felt herself becoming more of the woman she wanted to be.

Amanda kissed Moon on the forehead first. It was a kiss that had an audible smack to it. Rather chaste, actually. Then Amanda kissed Moon's closed eyelids. She kissed them very softly and very slowly and intimately. She was in no hurry. The girl was not a meal that should be devoured quickly, in great hurried gulps. She was a delightful entrée that must be slowly and lovingly treasured nibble by nibble, bite by bite. She was to be savored.

Amanda kissed the tip of Moon's nose, and the girl smiled.

Amanda looked to the side. Blade had his recently satisfied cock in his hand. It wasn't quite yet in a full-on erection, not having achieved all its formidable dimensions, but Amanda had no doubt that soon it would return to her vaunted expectations.

He recovers quickly, she thought, once again impressed with the warrior's amazing virility. *Doesn't he ever get enough?*

She wasn't at all certain what she should think about her lover's extraordinary ability.

She had delayed the ultimate delight as long as she possibly could. Moving her hands so that she held Moon's face lightly between her palms, Amanda paused a moment to look at the girl. Had there ever been a maiden who looked so pure, so innocent, so lovely? Amanda knew that Moon was a widow, so she certainly wasn't pure. And the erotic things that Moon had introduced her to the other night certainly proved that she was anything but naïve about matters of the flesh. But still, there was something in her character, something in her demeanor, that gave off an aura of the most gentle, sweet innocence that Amanda could imagine.

When Amanda touched her lips to Moon's, kissing the girl gently and passionately, she very nearly started to cry. The kiss itself was the very embodiment of tenderness. It was feminine desire without so much as a hint of masculinity.

Amanda's emotions quickly evolved when Moon parted her lips. Then she used the tip of her tongue to slide it back and forth between Amanda's lips. Amanda pressed her mouth more firmly against the girl's, and a moment later she had Moon's tongue deep in her mouth.

Their kiss lasted just short of an eternity, but that still wasn't long enough to quench Amanda's thirst. She kissed the girl's throat for several seconds, then went right back to her mouth, feasting on Moon's lips, squirming her naked body so that their breasts pressed against each other's.

Amanda kissed Moon's throat again, but instead of returning to her mouth, she kissed her way slowly and sensually downward. She used the tip of her tongue to trace the line of Moon's collar bone, then licked her way farther southward until she was at the sloping upper edge of a tawny breast that seemed to be all but begging to be orally caressed.

Blade said softly, "That's so beautiful."

The sound of Blade's voice heightened Amanda's arousal. Knowing that he was there and watching everything that she was doing added fuel to the inferno of her passion. He wasn't merely accepting what she was doing with Moon, he was approving of it. His encouragement made her passion burn more brightly. Exhibitionism had come to life in Amanda's soul, and she embraced it with all her heart.

Exhibitionism also made her want to give Blade a show that he'd never forget for the rest of his life.

Using the tip of her tongue, she circled Moon's erect left nipple, coming close to be never quite touching it. She heard the girl make a sound in her throat that was a strange and highly erotic mixture of frustration and passion.

Amanda tilted her face upward. She looked at Blade. His eyes were dark and glittering. His erection, still in his hand, was now fully formed. The sight of it made Amanda shiver.

"She has such a beautiful body, doesn't she?" Amanda asked rhetorically. "Look at how hard her nipples are."

She watched as Blade moistened his lips with the tip of his tongue and listened as he cleared his throat three times. He then said, "Suck on them. I think Moon would like that."

Amanda made a purring sound in her throat. It was a natural sound that came from her, one of carnal contentment, not one that was contrived or theatrical.

She looked into Moon's eyes. She was looking into them when her lips surrounded the girl's left nipple. Moon said something in a language that Amanda did not understand, though the mean was clear. Moon loved having her nipples sucked on as much as Amanda loved sucking on them.

Amanda released Moon's breast after some time, then used her tongue on Moon's navel, but not for long. Her ultimate goal was south of that delicious little belly button. After foolishly restricting herself, Amanda was anxious now to delight in a new and sumptuous form lovemaking.

She kissed Moon's lower abdomen, her lips now just inches above Moon's sex. Amanda could smell the girl's passion and knew that her nectar was flowing freely. The evidence of feminine desire heightened Amanda's confidence and gave her the courage to go into sexual territory that was foreign to her.

Amanda eased her arms from the underside to encircle Moon's slender thighs. She slipped the girl's lets upward until they were on her shoulders, and she could feel her heels against her back.

Amanda brought her fingertips to the petals of Moon's sex and gently separated them, revealing the pink inner flesh and the small, erotic clitoris that glistened with excitement.

I can make her climax again, Amanda thought, her confidence more solid now.

After several seconds of Amanda's deliberation, Moon said softly, "Please . . . Will you? Take me there again."

There was a smile on Amanda's lips as she brought her mouth to Moon's pussy. When her tongue eased between slick labia, Moon let out a cry of ecstasy, and her body flinched as though she'd been given a powerful electrical shock. She uttered a word that Amanda did not understand. Amanda decided it didn't matter. Moon's body was telling her everything she needed to know.

When she heard Blade let out a low groan of sexual desire, Amanda realized that she was doing exactly what she should be doing. She was embracing and fulfilling her own destiny, and she was just now realizing that.

Amanda captured Moon's clitoris between her lips and sucked lightly. The young woman arched her back, and Amanda followed her movements, never letting her lips leave contact with Moon's clitoris.

Moon was saying something, though Amanda didn't know what the words meant. All she was certain of was that the girl was pleased with what was being done to her—and that was all that really mattered to Amanda.

Moon soon became less frantic, her body no longer tensed and arched, and this allowed Amanda to more leisurely lick the girl's exceptionally responsive sex. Amanda took her time, licking up one petal, then down the other. Each time she licked upward, she caught Moon's erect clitoris between her lips, licked it for a moment, then sucked on it.

As she went about pleasuring Moon, Amanda developed a rather objective, utterly scientific mindset. Though she enjoyed orally caressing Moon, she studied the girl's responses to what she was doing rationally, wanting to discover what it was that she enjoyed the most, and what places she most enjoyed being caressed.

She likes it best when I suck on her button, Amanda thought as she drew a slightly firmer suction on the girl's clitoris. *She really likes it a lot.*

Amanda, palm upward, slipped a single finger deep into Moon as she used her lips on the girl's clitoris. This caused moon to flinch sharply, and once again arch her back.

She liked that a lot. A finger inside her and my lips surrounding her clitoris, Amanda thought. *I should do this to her often. Very often.*

She almost smiled at the awareness but didn't. Her lips were too busy to curl into a smile.

She could hear Blade's rapid, deep breathing. Though she knew he was a man of great experience, she suspected that the drama she and Moon were performing for him while perhaps not being unprecedented was still profoundly arousing to his senses.

Amanda took her mouth away from Moon's pussy. She looked Blade directly in the eyes. She said, "She's delicious. And since you've already given me so much, I don't want to be selfish. Would you like me to share her with you?"

Blade nodded instantly. This didn't surprise Amanda in the least.

Though he was a big man, Blade could move with the kind of fluid grace that made Amanda think of a stalking puma, moving silently and with serious intent. He moved into position beside her. Moon had to spread her slender thighs wider apart to accommodate the two of them.

"I know I'm repeating myself," Amanda said in a sultry whisper that was just loud enough to reach Moon, "but she's delicious. She tastes like rain drops at dawn."

Amanda was endlessly pleased when Blade took the time to kiss her before he turned his lusty skills upon Moon. She watched intently as he used his lips and tongue on the girl and listened to Moon's moans and sighs of ecstasy with a serious student's rapt intensity.

A thick lock of Blade's ebony hair fell over his face, obscuring Amanda's view of what he was doing to Moon. She reached out and tucked the errant lock behind his ear.

He's the most beautiful man I've ever seen, she thought.

Moon whispered words in a language Amanda did not understand, though she could tell they were words of praise.

He does that better than I do, Amanda thought, cringing at the unpleasant awareness. *Of course he does. He's given that kind of delight to more women than I can imagine, and all I've ever done is tasted Moon.*

The sense of being inadequate crept into Amanda's consciousness, and she immediately realized that she had to banish such emotions. Nothing good could come from that train of thought.

"You've had enough," she said with a certain catty inflection in her tone. "It's my turn now."

Amanda pulled Moon's leg more securely over her left shoulder, then began devouring the girl's sex with a skill that was improving by the second, and an enthusiasm that was shooting like a meteor.

Her lips were surrounding Moon's clitoris when the girl experienced her next climax. Blade was kissing Amanda on the ear, his tongue probing erotically, as Moon climaxed on Amanda's mouth.

"Stop . . . stop," Moon said when her orgasm had finished, speaking English for the first time in quite a while.

Amanda, now cognizant of what it was like to climax upon

a greedy, ravenous mouth, immediately pulled back from the girl. There was such a thing as too much of a good thing.

"You've got her juices almost to your ears," Blade said with utter delight in his voice.

When Amanda looked at him, the gleam in his eyes was everything that she could hope for.

"I adore you. You know that, right?" Amanda said to Blade.

He kissed her hungrily, deeply, then pulled away so that she could look into his eyes.

"I can taste Moon's delight when I kiss you," Blade said softly, the timber of his voice deep, the intonation shockingly honest and evocative. "You're the sexiest woman I've ever known, and I love you more than either of us can possibly imagine."

Amanda took in the full impact of Blade's words, and she felt a sensation inside her soul that she'd never felt before. She kissed him softly, then turned her face and kissed the inside of Moon's velvety soft copper-hued thigh.

"I want you so much, but I don't want to be selfish with my treasure," Amanda said to Blade. She cleared her throat and summoned up the courage to say the words that she knew had to be spoken. "I want you, but it's Moon who needs you now. Right now, at this very moment, she needs all that you can do for her." Amanda moved the few inches that separated her from Blade and kissed him on the mouth twice in quick succession. "She's such a lovely girl, she's had such a very difficult time, and she needs you so much."

Blade smiled at Amanda, then turned his head and kissed Moon's pussy, though he did it very briefly before he kissed her abdomen. He began moving upward, kissing her stomach, then her breasts. Amanda eased the girl's thigh off her shoulder, and moved to the side, giving the lovers room to do what was necessary, while affording herself a prime seat in the theater of sex that was about to play out right before her eyes.

"Guide me," Blade said moments later to Amanda when his powerful, sweaty body was properly positioned between Moon's thighs.

Amanda, kneeling at Moon's hip, immediately curled her fingers around the thickly veined shaft of Blade's arousal, then moved him so that she could rub the crown of his erection against the shimmering lips of Moon's pussy. For a moment she envied the girl. She was well aware of the ecstasy Moon was about to experience.

Amanda watched as the man she loved pushed his hips downward. The head of his magnificent cock pried apart the sex lips of a beautiful young widow who Amanda hardly knew but had experienced shockingly intimate sex with.

Moon gasped. It was an ambiguous sound. Amanda didn't know what to make of it.

He's so big, Amanda thought. *And she's so little.*

It surprised Amanda when she realized that she was more concerned with Moon's possible discomfort than she was with the fact that Blade was having sex with someone other than herself.

She watched, unblinking and hardly breathing, as Blade's erection slipped smoothly between spreading, glistening labia. Blade pushed half his length into Moon, then stopped. When he retreated, his withdrawal was slow and deliberate. Amanda knew exactly how blissful it was to experience Blade's erection first filling her body, then sliding out of it. The man, she realized, was a master at all things that touched the senses.

Amanda thought, *The next time he'll give her everything he's got.*

It surprised Amanda that, as she watched Blade's cock burying into the girl's body, she didn't feel resentment or jealousy or any negative emotions whatsoever.

Moon needs this, Amanda decided. *She needs Blade, at least for tonight. At least for right now. It would be selfish of me to keep him to myself.*

Amanda combed her fingers through Blade's raven hair. She heard herself say "kiss me" but it seemed to her that someone else had spoken the words. When Blade had reached full insertion, he turned his face toward her. She kissed his lips firmly, easing her tongue into his mouth. She heard Moon's soft sigh of contentment, and Amanda knew then with absolute certainty that she was doing the right thing. This night was meant to be. It was ordained by powers Amanda could sense but could not entirely comprehend.

She was still kissing Blade when he began moving his hips with a smooth, steady rhythm which Amanda herself had experienced and taken glory in.

Moon was whispering words of praise. Amanda didn't know what the words actually meant, but Moon's tone told Amanda everything that she needed to know. Passion speaks a universal language that all lovers understand. This was something that Amanda was just now learning.

Blade pushed full-length into Moon, then he moved his hips from side to side, firmly grinding himself against the girl. He turned his face away from Amanda, then lowered himself sufficiently to kiss Moon on the forehead, then nose, then mouth.

His gentleness excited Amanda. She'd never met a man of such controlled power.

He's so beautiful, Amanda thought as she watched the man she loved kissing a beautiful young widow of infinite charm.

It took a moment for Amanda to realize that she was touching herself intimately, the pads of her right hand pressing against her clitoris, moving in a very pleasing circular motion. She was touching herself precisely as she liked to be touched. No one could know her body and desires quite as well as she did herself.

Amanda felt the erotic pleasure flowing through her veins. She stopped using all her fingers and began using only the pad of her middle finger against her clitoris to concentrate the sensations she was feeling. She was a woman who knew from experience what she was doing. And she did it well. Extremely well. Her smile was beatific.

Moon's thigh now obscured Amanda's view of Blade's cock sliding in and out of her, and though Amanda thought briefly of complaining — her voyeurism was becoming something quite more than just a mild fetish — she kept her words to herself. It wasn't easy for her to not complain. With Blade and Moon now in her life, indulging her desires had become a necessity, not a luxury.

She watched as Blade and Moon kissed and discovered that it was more disconcerting to her to see them kissing than it was to watch Blade's erection gliding into Moon's welcoming and oh-so-eager body.

She forced the unpleasant awareness out of her thoughts with an almost vicious forcefulness and turned her concentration and emotions on the things that gave her pleasure.

Things like touching herself, and the insistent throbbing of her clitoris as she rubbed it with her middle finger, using just the right amount of pressure to ensure the maximum amount of delight which, she was certain, would soon lead to satisfaction. Self-administered, but delightful just the same. She decided there was nothing wrong with being self-sufficient and taking a hands-on approach to problem solving.

Amanda watched as Blade kissed Moon on the mouth. It was easy to see that their mouths were open, and that tongues were most definitely involved in the pleasuring. But then, quite suddenly, Blade ended the kiss and straightened his arms so that his chest was no longer on the girl's lovely breasts. He looked at Amanda, and the fire in his dark eyes was enough to make her feel that strange combination of primal fear and arousal that only Blade could inspire. He had taught her that terror and ecstasy could coexist.

"Kiss her," Blade said in that decisive way that declared only bad things would happen if his orders weren't followed immediately and to the letter. "Kiss her now . . . and make her feel it." He paused a moment, then added, "I want to see that she feels it deep down in her soul."

Amanda waited, but only long enough for Blade to resume the back-and-forth movements of his hips. She brought her mouth to Moon's. When they kissed, Amanda felt a sense of collegial completion that she'd never before experienced. As she kissed Moon, she felt closer to the young widow than she'd ever experience with any female in her life. She said a silent prayer of thanks to whatever celestial powers had brought Moon into her life.

After long seconds of tongue dancing against tongue and going from mouth to mouth, Amanda ended the kiss and leaned back on her knees, sitting on her heels.

There wasn't an inch of her body that wasn't aroused. She slipped a single finger between the lips of her pussy, and the pleasure she gave herself was intense.

Amanda found it impossible to maintain a steady, intimate kiss with Moon. The girl's slender body was rocking from the steady pounding that Blade was giving her. Judging by the sighs, moans, and gasps of delight that were almost continuously coming from Moon—even while she had Amanda's tongue deep in her mouth—Blade was giving her everything she wanted.

Blade's arms were straight beneath him to keep his upper body off Moon as his fierce arousal plundered Moon's passion-starved body. This gave Amanda room to caress Moon's breasts, then slide her hand even farther down, over the flat stomach then continuing on its journey.

Amanda searched for and quickly found Moon's clitoris.

She used her middle two fingers on the slick center of all the girl's desires. Within seconds, as Blade continued pumping into Moon and Amanda simultaneously caressed her clitoris with a firm, vigorous, circular motion, Moon climaxed. It seemed to Amanda to be a very powerful orgasm. The young widow's slender body shook and shivered as Blade plunged downward and then retreated upward, and Amanda danced her tongue with Moon's.

Through clenched teeth, Blade groaned and said softly "I can't go much longer. Not without . . ."

The last word remained unspoken, but the people in the tepee knew what hadn't been said.

Amanda ended her kiss with Moon, raised up enough to kiss Blade quickly, then said to him, "You've been generous long enough. It's your turn to find paradise."

As though her words had flipped an orgasmic switch inside Blade, he thrust into Moon's precious body one last time, then withdrew completely. His cock was as hard as stone, and glistening with Moon's juices.

Amanda acted instantly, wrapping her fingers around the slick shaft of Blade's cock. She moved her fist back and forth over its entire length while great gushes of cum erupted from the slit in the crown, leaving rivers of cream from Moon's breasts to her belly button.

Incongruous of the intensity of the moment, once Blade had finished with his orgasm, he slumped to the side and began laughing. Once he started laughing, Moon and Amanda joined him.

CHAPTER ELEVEN

They headed out after Dog and his men at dawn. Blade had hoped Amanda would oversleep, but the spirits weren't kind. When he saw her, dressed in doeskins and with braided blonde hair, he found himself questioning his earlier decision to return Amanda to the white man's villages. She was a teacher, and one of the main reasons for the Northern Comanche's success despite their numbers was because of their literacy, which was now into the third generation of the tribe.

And, of course, there was that oft-repeated declaration of ownership the previous evening that Blade couldn't forget uttering. Amanda hadn't mentioned it, and for that he was grateful. But he had spent well over a decade keeping his status as bachelor firmly fixed in place. He accomplished that by making a point of never making claims of matrimony.

What he said to Amanda was a staggering departure from the status quo . . . but was it inaccurate?

Forcing thoughts of Amanda from his mind, he patted Tikki's neck and resumed concentrating on following the three-days-old hoof prints left by Dog's band of murderers.

* * *

How far ahead do you think they are?" Sheriff Benson asked.

Blade got down on one knee to more closely inspect the hoof print. "Twelve hours. Just twelve hours, and they're moving slow."

"Why do you suppose that is?"

Blade shrugged his broad shoulders. "They don't think they're being followed. But we've got to be careful. Dog is just as vicious as his older brother was, and he's a lot more cunning. Blue Elk was their leader only because he was older. And he was more vicious than any man I've ever met."

"What kind of men are we after?"

The right side of Blade's mouth pulled upward in a bitter smile. "The worst. They kill for sport, and they don't make allowances for women and children." He looked at Sheriff Benson, trying to see past the man's gruff exterior. "You should know that Blue Elk and Dog watched their parents get slaughtered by your cavalry about ten or twelve years ago. I'll grant you those brothers are human monsters, but they got an early education in barbarity from the white man."

"That's no excuse for what they've done. It's not important."

"Maybe not now," Blade replied. "But it was damned sure important at one time."

There was less than thirty minutes of sunlight left. Blade pulled Tikki to a stop and twisted in his saddle to look at Sheriff Benson.

"How far ahead are they?" the lawman asked.

"Eight hours, tops. We'll stop here and set up camp. We don't want to stumble upon them in the dark."

The sheriff nodded and turned his horse around to give the directions to the rest of the posse. Amanda, having heard the exchange, smiled to herself. She had noticed how, during the course of the day, Blade had become the leader of the posse. Even Sheriff Benson, who clearly didn't like having to deal with Indians, followed Blade's orders without complaint.

They ate beans and buffalo jerky that night. Though the posse all had their blankets arranged near the small campfire,

Despite the rather disapproving looks from the sheriff, Blade and Amanda put their blankets off to the west about twenty yards. Blade had earlier commented on the surreptitious, covetous looks the posse members had been casting in her direction. Though she said nothing, she was thrilled with Blade's protectiveness toward her.

"How are you feeling?" Blade asked, sitting in the prairie grass, chewing on tangy dried buffalo meat.

"Fine," Amanda replied. She blushed a little. "Actually, that's a little white lie. I'm sore, but I've never felt such a wonderful pain in my life."

Blade's dark eyes turned away from her guiltily. "I shouldn't have made love to you that last time. If I'd stopped, you wouldn't be hurting now."

"Perhaps. But I wouldn't have experienced the pleasure, either."

She bit off a small piece of jerked buffalo. Her legs were folded to the side, covered by the simple doeskin dress she had learned to appreciate for its practicality. She looked at Blade, enjoying the stark perfection of his profile, fully understanding why he was in such demand by women without regard to the color of their skin.

Memories of watching Moon taking his cock into her mouth, of seeing her writhing in passion as he labored above her, flittered across the surface of her mind, and Amanda shivered. She was not unhappy that she had shared Blade with Moon. It was just something that took some getting used to.

"Tell me what you're thinking," Blade said.

She suddenly found it uncomfortable to look into his dark, fathomless eyes. "Moon needs you. She said I was being selfish by keeping you all to myself. I . . . I purposely invited her to join us so that you could pleasure her. And I've done things with her that I've never told you. You pleasured her with that devilish tongue of yours, and you had me pleasure her with mine . . . but you didn't really make love to her, did you? Not like you did to me." She cleared her throat nervously. "She's the one who is staying. She's part of your tribe . . . your family . . . Shouldn't she . . ."

Blade sighed wearily. "Yes, I know my obligations are to her." He sighed again. "You've got to understand that your customs and ours are not at all alike."

Amanda's lifted her gaze. "What's it like to be in such demand as a lover? What's it like knowing you can have practically any woman you want, whenever you want her?"

"It's not really like that."

"I suspect it is." Amanda felt a nebulous emotion welling up inside her, one she couldn't identify. She was as susceptible to Blade's easy charm as all the other women within the sphere of his influence. "When I'm gone," she continued, but then her throat tightened, cutting off her words.

"Let's not talk about that now."

"When I'm gone," she said, forcing herself to say the critical words, "will you take Moon as your wife? She needs a husband, and it is so obvious that she's completely smitten with you."

"It's my obligation to see that she has food and shelter, but that doesn't mean I'm going to take her as my wife."

"With your hunting skills, and your sexual skills, you could easily support three or four wives." Her tone had suddenly become colored with a kind of peevish petulance, but she seemed powerless to stop it. "You could have four or five wives now that I think of it. Just imagine, every night could be a veritable orgy for you."

"It's not like that."

"Yes, it is. It's exactly like that. You just won't admit it." Amanda stood abruptly. Night would descend over the land in just minutes. "Come take a walk with me."

Blade got to his feet, let Sheriff Benson know he was taking a short walk, then returned to Amanda. He held his rifle in the crook of his right arm and the revolver was in the holster at his left hip. She could tell from his posture and the ease with which he held the weapons that — if circumstances warranted it — he could be a savagely dangerous man. She understood why the Northern Comanche had chosen him to be their war chief and why young men would follow him into battle. He exuded confidence without saying a word, and in doing so, he inspired confidence in others.

They walked in silence, moving away from the camp. When Amanda's hand bumped Blade's, he slipped his fingers around her hand, and she was nearly brought to tears. It felt so natural to be holding hands with Blade, but she couldn't help but wonder how much she'd miss that touch when she was in town once again, an unmarried schoolmarm that nobody would ever believe could be swept away by an ungovernable passion.

"It's been a while since I've been in this territory," Blade said quietly, distracting Amanda from her troubling thoughts. With his rifle, he pointed to a stream perhaps a hundred yards away, visible with the moonlight shining off its slowly moving surface. "Three years ago, we got into quite a skirmish with a Kiowa war party right near that bend in the stream. We ended up with two of my men wounded." His lips pressed into a thin line, and he shook his head. "I hate it whenever my men get hurt."

"What happened to the Kiowa war party?" Amanda asked, though she wasn't at all certain she wanted an answer.

"We killed nine the first day. They retreated, then attacked again in the morning." His voice was distant as he recalled the battle. "They lost two or three more before just riding away and leaving us alone."

Blade shrugged his powerful shoulders and combed his

fingers though his hair. She could see, then, the burden of leadership he carried with him always. He was more than just a warrior; Broken Blade saw the entire Northern Comanche as his personal family, and as such, he was responsible for them. She was beginning to understand the totality of this emotion, and the more of it she understood, the greater her respect for Blade.

"You worry about your people all the time, don't you?" she asked.

A flashing grin displayed startling white teeth. "Not all the time. Sometimes I worry about you."

He eased his hand around the back of Amanda's neck. For several seconds, their gazes locked and held, then Blade slowly bent toward her. But before his lips reached hers, he stood upright again.

"What's wrong?" She was *always* in the mood to receive Blade's kisses.

"You're already sore," Blade explained. "I don't want to compound my guilt."

"You've saved my life, taught me passion, and have never, ever done anything to me to feel guilty about. So, give me that kiss you just shied away from, or I really will feel poorly treated."

He kissed her then, and her first thought was that she shouldn't succumb so thoroughly and so quickly to a simple kiss. Except no kiss from Blade could be considered either simple or harmless, and her body, though tender from sexual excess, instantly warmed to the possibility of his passion.

"Stop this now," Blade said when that kiss finally ended. "You told me yourself that you're sore."

Amanda eased her hand beneath the front flap of Blade's breechclout. Beneath the soft leather, his burgeoning shaft jumped. When she squeezed, he uttered a soft groan of pleasure, and his cock instantly lengthened.

"Stop it." There was equivocation in his tone.

"That's what your mouth is saying to me, but it isn't what your body's saying . . . or wanting." She squeezed again, and this time there could be no denying he was growing. "I may have overindulged, but you obviously haven't had enough."

Amanda was feeling more confident in her sexuality than she'd ever dreamed possible. She began tugging at the buckle to his gun belt with hands that trembled from excitement but not fear. "Help me, Blade."

"You don't have to do this."

"Yes, I do. I'll go crazy if I don't."

Blade unbuckled his belt, then untied the braided sash holding up his breechclout. The buckskin fell to the ground between his feet, and the length of his magnificent cock swung out toward her. Although not yet fully aroused, he was already impressive in stature.

"Has anyone ever told you that you've got a beautiful cock?" Amanda asked as she sank to her knees. She held him in both hands, angling her head back on her shoulders to look up into his face. "I'm sure women have, so please don't answer that last question. I shouldn't have asked it. I know the answer, but I'm trying to pretend I don't." She sighed. "Let me have my illusions."

Blade chuckled at Amanda's sauciness until she eased her lips over the crown of his erection and put her tongue in motion against the underside of the head of his cock. As she began nodding to and fro, she looked up at the man she adored, and whose cock was currently filling her mouth.

In his buckskin shirt and leggings but without his breechclout, only his groin was exposed. Blade seemed to her then to be the personification of untamed manliness, a warrior who was utterly dangerous and completely exciting to every nerve that made a woman feel like a woman.

She moaned to let Blade know that she loved being on her

knees before him. She was responsible for his flaring erection. Knowing she had created such a response from a man as beautiful to the eyes as Blade made her confidence soar and her clitoris start to tingle.

Amanda slipped a hand inside her dress. Touching her delicate labia, she found she was already wet, and though better judgment suggested she be satisfied with selflessly giving satisfaction to Blade, his allure was such that she needed to feel him inside her.

Leaning back and releasing him from her oral embrace, she looked up at him. She offered a soft smile as she sat back, kicked her legs out in the grass, and raised the front skirt of her doeskin dress.

"Make love to me, Blade," she whispered. "Not for too long . . . but I've got to feel you inside me."

Blade argued that he shouldn't, but he seemed as incapable of resisting her as she was of resisting him. And though it did, in fact, hurt to accept his dimensions into her tender pussy, it was worth it, though, when the white hot shards of her orgasm struck like lightning. Her satisfaction was complete when she heard his growl of pleasure as he released his semen deep inside her.

Afterward, Blade was resting his weight on his elbows as Amanda smoothed his hair out of his eyes. He was still atop her.

"You're mine," he whispered. He dipped his head down and brushed a kiss to the tip of her nose. "And we've got to find a husband for Moon Will Shine."

Amanda's heart skipped a beat. Or three. Not daring to trust her own senses, she queried, "Pardon?"

"Maybe I'm getting the order all mixed up, but I want a husband for Moon because I want you as my bride. My only bride. For now, she'll be ours, but in the future, she should have a husband she doesn't have to share."

Hot tears formed in her eyes, but she refused to shed them. "Are you asking me to marry you?"

"Yes. Badly, but yes." He kissed her forehead. "Will you marry me?"

"Only me. No other wives?"

"Only you. No other wives. As soon as it can be arranged." Blade's expression was stone serious.

She didn't want the tears to flow, but they wouldn't be checked.

Blade groaned. "And now I've made you cry."

"Tears of joy." She wiped the tears away. "Yes, I want to marry you. I don't know what customs you follow to get married, and I don't care. So long as eventually I'm your *only* wife, I don't care about anything else." A sob caught in her throat. "But I'm going to miss having Moon in our tent. We've got to find someone truly special for her. Promise me, whoever he is, he'll be truly special."

"He'll be as special as Moon. I promise you that."

They found Dog and his men the next day. Amanda, peering through powerful field glasses, confirmed their identities as the men who had attacked the train. As the posse got ready to attack the larger force, Blade explained to Amanda that she had to stay far from the battlefield. When she resisted, he said, "No wife of mine is going into battle, so don't argue with me."

She would have argued, but the word 'wife' sounded so magnificent that she was left speechless.

While Amanda could not see the gunfight that followed less than an hour later, she could hear it. Each new volley of gunfire made her heart seize up. She prayed to God for the safety of the man who would be her husband. Then, not quite certain of Blade's spirituality, she prayed to any gods who would listen and might protect the man she loved.

Dog and his men knew that if they were ever captured,

they'd be tried in a court of law and hanged. They had nothing to lose by fighting to the bitter end, and that's exactly what they did. To a man, they were buried in that prairie. Sheriff Benson's posse lost two men, and four more were wounded. Blade had been bloodied when a bullet grazed his thigh, and though the wound had caused the loss of quite a bit of blood, it was still only superficial, though Amanda tended to him as though he was sitting at death's door.

It was some weeks later that, as far as Blade was concerned, the man was awfully young to already be a colonel in the Army. He could be thirty. Maybe. Maybe a few years older than that. Or younger. But he was a damned handsome lad, with good shoulders that could carry responsibility, and the kind of hips and thighs that said he'd spent more hours on horseback than most men in their sixties. And he was handsome in a Nordic sort of way, with blond hair that came down over his uniform's collar, and a down-turned mustache that was bold enough to suggest that he had a certain theatrical flair to him that whispered not so quietly that he liked to make bold statements now and then. He seemed like the kind of man who could always back up those bold statements.

His name was Colonel John Samuelson, and he and the men he commanded were searching for deserters who had robbed a bank and killed three people at the bank before they made their getaway.

"They didn't get more than a couple hundred dollars," the colonel said to Blade. He kept his voice low because Amanda and Moon were standing nearby, and, apparently, he was enough of a gentleman to not want them to hear such disturbing news. "I've got to find them. These men must be brought to justice."

Blade looked at the man and liked everything about him.

It wasn't important that he was handsome. What was important was that he had a sense of duty, that he knew right from wrong, and that he understood the concept of justice. These were the principles that Blade lived by, and it impressed him that the young colonel did, too.

"Around these parts, it's said that if the man named Broken Blade can't track a man, then that man's got to be a ghost," the colonel said. "I need a man like that to help me see that justice is served. That means I need you."

Bladed was getting mighty tired of being in the mix of seeing that men who deserved nothing but a hangman's noose got what they earned, but it seemed that the universe had other plans for him.

He looked over at Amanda and Moon. They were standing close together, talking in whispers. He wondered what they were talking about.

When he looked back at the handsome, young colonel, Blade found him — as he had several times in the past hour — looking at Moon. Looking at her with an expression of something akin to rapture on his face. One would have thought he was looking at an angel.

Moon's beautiful, so naturally she draws attention, Blade thought as he studied the colonel's profile. *The colonel's nothing less than mystified with her.*

"Colonel . . ." Blade said, feeling the need to pull the young man back into the conversation and out of his romantic reverie.

"Sorry. I was just thinking about something," he said. Then, after a moment, he added what Blade knew was a lie. "Lots of problems in the barracks right now. When there are deserters, it looks bad for everyone."

Liar. You're thinking about Moon, and only about her, Blade thought with utter delight. *An ambitious young colonel, eh? And handsome, to boot. He looks like a man who could make Moon happy.*

"Perhaps we should have something to eat?" Blade said

with deceptive nonchalance, giving the young colonel a smile. "You don't mind me calling you John, do you?"

"No," the colonel said, clearly flustered "Of course not."

"We'll eat in my tepee," Blade said casually, taking the uniformed officer by the elbow. "I live there with my fiancée and my brother's widow. I'll introduce you to them."

When Blade looked at Moon, he saw that the girl's beautiful chocolate brown gaze never left the colonel for even a second.

The snow was falling when Amanda's water broke three weeks before her due date. She was in a tepee at the time, giving English grammar lessons to Northern Comanche children. The tribal elders all agreed that she was a wonderful teacher, and that her influence in calming Broken Blade's profligate ways was a blessing from the spirits.

The End

ABOUT THE AUTHOR

Robin Gideon is the author of over 50 novels and novellas in paperback form and for e-publishers. She is currently writing erotic action-adventure stories starring the secret agent Svetlana Simonov exclusively for eXtasy Books. She was the featured author on the nationally syndicated TV series CBS Sunday Morning. She loves hearing from her readers, and can be reached at: robin.gideon@ymail.com.

www.ingramcontent.com/pod-product-compliance
Lightning Source LLC
Chambersburg PA
CBHW060616130626
46555CB00002B/527